1

SARAH

The first flakes of snow were dancing in the light of the streetlamp as Sarah Wilson flipped over the little sign on the door of the Harbour Café, letting the tiny Highland town of Applemore know she was open for business.

It was still dark at 7.30 a.m., because midwinter days in the far north of the Scottish Highlands were short. The inky black sky was present both at the start of her day and at the end of it, when she flipped the sign back the other way and closed the door, hanging up her apron for the night.

There was a nice symmetry to it, like being wrapped in a velvety blanket of stars. Beyond the metal rails of the harbour the sea shifted like a liquid shadow, and if you screwed up your eyes and focused really hard, you could almost make out somewhere in the distance the dark shapes of the islands.

"Fancy talk," she could hear her mother saying, with a fond tut of disapproval. She'd always been the daydreamer, airy-fairy to her brother Tor's grounded practicality.

There were worse places to be, Sarah thought, as she moved through the little café, placing a fresh tealight on each of the

A HIGHLAND CHRISTMAS

RACHAEL LUCAS

*For Jude, who loves Hallmark Christmas movies
just as much as I do.*

six wooden tables. The air was already filling with the scent of the gingerbread cookies she'd started earlier that morning, and a little bell sounded in the back kitchen reminding her that it was time to take the second batch of sourdough out of the oven.

Her arms ached from stretching and folding the heavy dough, and her feet were tired from standing up for hours and hours every day. But soon the first customers would arrive and she'd forget that, caught up in the ever-changing daily bustle of life here in the middle of the village.

"Morning," sang Chloe, her assistant, a few minutes later. She arrived like a whirlwind, flicking on the radio and filling the café with the sound of Christmas music. She threw off her coat, hanging it up on the rack by the back door, revealing a striped top with a sequinned penguin in a Santa hat. Chloe was indispensable, and lived for the holiday season, rolling straight from Halloween outfits into full tinsel mode on the first of November.

"If I have to listen to Mariah Carey one more time," Sarah said, lifting a rolling pin in mock threat.

"You love it really." Chloe draped a piece of red tinsel around Sarah's neck and reached for her own apron, which was hanging freshly laundered on the hook by the door. She took a band from around her wrist and tied her blonde hair back in a bun, ready for work.

Sarah rolled her eyes and groaned. "There are many things I appreciate about Christmas, but that song is not one of them."

They'd compromised – with Chloe decorating the café with hand-made paper chains as soon as she could – that Christmas music was for December only. Even so, Sarah was quietly longing for New Year's Day and the peace that it would bring.

Humming, Chloe wiped down the metal worktop and pulled out the white dishes, setting out the spice-scented gingerbread cookies in a neat line.

"Hello-oo," came a familiar voice as the little bell jingled, letting them know that their first customer had arrived. From now on, they'd have a constant stream of people popping in to collect their daily bread, before the café visitors took over.

Sarah dusted off her apron and headed out front, where Dolina Allen was standing at the counter with her green anorak zipped up tightly. Her grey hair was dusted with tiny snowflakes and her cheeks pink from the cold.

"Morning Dolina, you're early today." Sarah slid the plate of cookies onto the glass-fronted cabinet, where they joined the rows of freshly baked sourdough loaves and the glossy iced buns she'd finished earlier.

Dolina brushed some snow from the shoulders of her coat and pursed her lips, frowning as she surveyed the shelves. She did this every day, despite the fact that – having been one of Sarah's mother's best friends, who'd visited the café without fail every day since it opened – the range had barely altered. Every spring she'd remark in surprise at the hot cross buns, and every winter she'd coo with delight over the *lebkuchen* and spiced cookies as if they were a surprise. *It was*, Sarah thought, *her funny little way of showing her support.*

"Those gingerbreads look very good today, Sarah. Isobel would be proud of you." Dolina gave a little nod.

Sarah glanced out of the window to see the snow was falling more heavily now, the flakes thickening and starting to heap up against the metal harbour railing.

"Looks like we might get a white Christmas."

Dolina pushed her glasses up her nose and followed Sarah's gaze. "Aye, we might do. That'll be nice for the kiddies. I thought I'd get organised early, and get the wee ones some of your gingerbread before they all get sold out." She fished in her bag for her purse. "I've got the grandchildren nursery because Jenny's working up at the Farm Shop all day, and I'm looking after Rilla's little Kitty as well."

"Three cookies, then?" Sarah said, reaching for a paper bag.

"Oh no," Dolina laughed. "Five. I want one, and Jenny deserves a treat after being on her feet all day." She gave her a searching look, the lines between her brows deepening as she frowned. "How are you doing?"

"Good thanks," Sarah said out of habit.

"No' working too hard?"

"It's Christmas," Sarah said, laughing as she flipped over the bag to seal the edges and passed it over. "And Applemore's not just busy in the summer these days, we seem to be getting tourists all year round."

"Aye, I hear the hotel's fully booked. Ever since they got that fancy new chef, Harry Robertson's been rushed off his feet."

"Well, whatever it is, I'm not complaining." Sarah waited as Dolina rifled in her purse for a ten-pound note.

"Here you go. Mind and have a rest," Dolina said, meeting her eyes for a moment. "Your mum wouldn't want you running yourself into the ground running this place."

"It's not going to run itself."

"True enough." Dolina put the cookies into her shopping bag and looked up again. "But she'd not want you running yourself into the ground. You could have a little break after the holidays. I'm sure Chloe could run the place for you."

Chloe popped her head round the side of the door, eyebrows waggling. "I'm waiting for my chance, Dolina," she said with a grin. "But this one is such a megalomaniac that she won't let go of the reins."

"Hardly." Sarah shook her head, laughing, as Dolina headed back out into the snow, holding the door open as two of the burly workers from the forestry made their way inside.

"Two coffees please, Sarah. And can we get six sausage rolls and a couple of pieces of that shortbread?"

Sarah's tired feet and the 3 a.m. wake up were forgotten in the rush. Before she knew it, it was half past ten.

"I am boiling." Chloe flapped her apron to try and create a breeze. "Can't believe they're all sitting there in jumpers."

They looked across the counter at the customers who were chatting away, every table now filled. Outside the window the snow was still falling, and a white fishing boat bobbed across a steely-grey sea, on the way back with a morning's catch. Inside, though, the café was warm and welcoming, each table decorated with a cute little miniature Christmas tree from the Beth's Flower Farm and a glowing tea-light flickering on the gingham tablecloth.

"They haven't been working as hard as we have. Coffee?"

"Please." Chloe got two mugs from the shelf. "Dolina's right, you know, you're overdoing it."

Sarah watched the beans dancing up and down as the grinder kicked into action, tamping the aromatic grounds into the holder and twisting it into place. She'd made count-less cups of coffee in the last three years, but even so, there was nothing like the feeling of that first cup after the rush. The machine hissed into action, and she leaned back, folding her arms and waiting.

"Ah, you read my mind."

Sarah turned at the familiar voice to see her twin brother standing there, his tall shape blocking the light from the window as he shook off the snow and pulled off his dark grey woollen beanie hat. As the local builder, he was just as over-stretched as his sister, working all year round. She watched as he ran a hand through his dark hair, pushing it up into untidy spikes.

"I was just telling your sister she needs a holiday. She hasn't stopped since the café opened," Chloe said, folding her arms.

Tor Wilson rubbed at the dark stubble on his jaw, meeting Sarah's hazel eyes with his dark brown ones. "I already told her." He shook his head disapprovingly.

She reached over for another mug.

"If I close up, we'll end up losing all our business to your mate Matt with his bakery up at the farm shop."

Tor grinned at her. "Unless he clones himself, there's no way he can keep up with demand. You two need each other. You need to organise it a bit better, get yourselves into a pattern so you can both have a rest."

Chloe passed her the milk, and a couple of moments later the three of them stood, each cupping a strong flat white coffee – their fuel to get them through the morning.

"Let's just hope that Applemore can manage without you now that Kenny's retired."

For years Tor had worked outside the village while Kenny – who'd been around so long it was a standing joke that he'd built most of Applemore – focused on the local work. But Kenny and his wife had taken early retirement, and Tor was juggling the business and bringing up his teenage son, Arran.

"I think the village will survive," Tor said drily. "You know as well as I do that half the 'Christmas emergencies' are anything but."

She grinned. "Oh yes. How could we forget the moment when you had to head out to one of Charlotte Fraser's holiday cottages in the middle of the Queen's Speech, and it turned out they needed a plumber instead."

"Or the time the roof caved in at the forestry office." Tor groaned. "I never heard the end of that one."

"Mum's last Christmas," Sarah said with a pang of sadness. "And you had to leave in the middle of pudding to go and sort it out."

"Yeah, if I'd known that, I might've let Kenny take the job. Funny how things happen, isn't it?"

"I can't believe that was four Christmases ago," Chloe sighed.

They all stood in silence for a moment, caught in memories. That had been the Christmas everything changed – rushing around to get the café open for the first time, not knowing that it would be the only café Christmas their mum would ever see. Laughing and joking as a family in Tor's big house up on the hill, not knowing that Tor and his wife, Victoria, had already agreed to split. Afterwards they'd admitted that they'd resolved to keep it quiet so they could have one more family Christmas – not knowing that their mum would be gone a few months later.

The year after that, they'd tried to pretend everything was normal, pasting on sad smiles and raising a toast to their mum as they went through the motions and attended the Christmas carol service around the Applemore tree. Last year they'd tried something different on Arran's suggestion and had pizza and watched Netflix all day... but that had felt even weirder. So, this year, with Arran spending Christmas in

Inverness with his mother, Tor had voted with his feet and booked a flight to Morrocco – after checking countless times that she'd cope on her own.

Sarah had waved an airy hand and told him she'd spend it with friends, but the truth was that she'd decided to just pretend it wasn't happening at all.

"Anyway," Sarah said, brightly, "I think it's good to mix things up a bit." She felt a pang of something that felt oddly like homesickness at the thought of her brother not being around and curled her fingers into her palms, pressing her nails in for a moment and blinking away a sting in her eyes. She picked up a cloth and turned to polish the chrome of the coffee machine for a moment, gathering herself.

"It'll be an experience," she heard Tor saying in the same slightly-too-cheerful tone.

She turned around and met his eyes for a second, raising a brow with a quick silent question.

Tor nodded once, as if to tell her that he'd be okay.

"When are you off?" Chloe, oblivious, snapped the leg off a gingerbread man and popped it into her mouth.

"Leaving first thing tomorrow morning."

"That soon?" Chloe whistled. "I feel like it's only five minutes since you decided."

"Yeah, and here we are. I'll be sunning myself in a souk by Wednesday."

"You might look a bit weird if you do," Sarah said, laughing. "A souk is a market. If you start stripping off, you're going to get some odd looks."

Chloe giggled as the door jingled, announcing a customer. "Make sure you've got Google Translate downloaded. Sounds like you're going to need it. Hi, what can I get you?"

She turned her smile to a tall man in wool coat with a turned-up collar, a scarf wrapped around his neck. Sarah turned back to Tor, slipping out from behind the counter to give her brother a hug.

"Come and see me later before you go?"

"Nah," said Tor, pulling back with a teasing laugh. "I was just going to disappear without saying goodbye."

"Very funny."

"I'll see you later."

2

JIM

"Coffee, please. Black."

Jim Fletcher hadn't factored in the Harbour Café being full at this time of day, but it was something to add to his research notes – if he could find somewhere to sit down and write them.

"Are you sitting in?" The blonde girl behind the counter looked at him with her brows raised in question. She was young and cheerful, with a streak of flour on the front of her dark blue apron. Behind her, a tall woman with dark salt-and-pepper curls tied back in a ponytail was cutting a tray of what looked like shortbread.

"That depends," he said, turning around to see the elderly couple who'd been sitting in the corner table by the window standing up and making to leave. The gentleman lifted his wife's coat, holding it up by the shoulders for her to put on, and Jim smiled.

"Looks like you're in luck," smiled the girl. "I'll bring it over to the table. Can I get you something to eat? Do you want some shortbread?"

The dark-haired woman looked up at them. She brushed back a dark curl that had fallen loose with the back of her forearm, smiling at him in a way that made him almost say yes despite the fact he'd just had a full breakfast at the Applemore Hotel.

Jim shook his head. "I already ate, unfortunately. It looks delicious."

"No problem." The blonde girl passed over the contactless pay unit and he held his phone to the side of the screen.

Sitting down at the table he pulled out his notebook and pen, pausing for a moment as he always did to take a mental note of his surroundings. The Harbour Café was busy, warm and bustling on a cold, snowy morning. Christmas decorations were strung from the heavy metal light fitting in the middle of the room, spanning out to each corner. They were old-fashioned paper style, crafted by hand and with love. Someone had put thought into the décor. He looked over as the girl headed his way with his coffee – a decently sized mug, he was glad to see. And she hadn't questioned his request for a black coffee, nor had she remarked on his New England accent. He accepted the mug with thanks and tapped his pen on the page for a moment before he started to write.

Harbour Café packed at 10 a.m. on a Tuesday – good sign.

Hand made decs – local artisans? (Art center outside the village)

No remark on US accent – tourists commonplace

On his travels through Scotland over the last couple of months, he'd found that his accent was as likely to open doors as it was to close them in his face. More than a few locals in Inverness had rolled their eyes as soon as he opened his mouth and he discovered that here in the Highlands not everyone was delighted at the prospect of yet another Yankee.

They tended to settle down, though, when he expanded on why he was really here – not to stake his claim as the great-great-great grandchild of the Laird of Auchtermory or some other equally exotic sounding place, but to research small towns. Their growth – or their decline – was his current fascination. The parallels between the Highlands and the little towns of New England were intriguing, and Applemore was the last on his list.

He took a first experimental sip of coffee, bracing himself – because if there was one thing he'd learned on his travels, it was that the Scottish Highlands might have many selling points – the purple hills that rose up to an ever-changing sky, silvery lochs that stretched out towards the horizon, not to mention the majestic stands of trees cut through with silent, empty roads that went on for miles – but their coffee could be hit or miss. He closed his eyes.

"Everything okay?"

Jim's eyes sprung open. The dark-haired woman was looking down at him with a curious expression on her face, a half-smile playing on her lips.

"Oh, sure. Yes. I was just" – he thought on the hop – "just thinking that what this coffee needs is a piece of that good-looking shortbread you offered me a moment ago."

"Good thinking." She folded the cloth she was holding and looked at him for a moment. "I'll bring it over. Two secs."

He watched as she dodged between the close-packed tables, noticing the way the navy-blue tie of her apron emphasised her waist which curved in from her ample hips. There was something about the way she moved that drew his eye, despite—

He shook his head. It was a long time since he'd noticed a woman. Strange then, that he couldn't quite bring himself to turn back to his notes, but watched as she moved behind the counter, making a joke to the blonde-haired girl as she fetched his order.

A moment later she returned, sliding the plate onto the table and cocking her head as she noticed his notebook.

"Are you a writer?"

He shook his head, pushing the book to one side as he looked up at her. She had a smattering of freckles across her nose, and wide hazel eyes fringed with thick lashes. No make up, as far as he could see, and he liked that her hair was streaked with silver-grey strands.

"No, nothing so exotic." With a finger, he adjusted the plate, turning it slightly so the little shortbread Christmas cookie was lined up straight. "I'm doing some research."

"In Applemore?" Her nose wrinkled in amusement. "What are you researching?"

"In short, small towns."

"Well, you've chosen a nice one. It's lovely at this time of year. Are you staying at the hotel?"

"I am, yes. I'll be here over the holiday."

"For the full Christmas experience."

He tipped his head in acknowledgement. "Something like that, yes."

Her eyes met his for a moment and it felt for a second as if something passed between the two of them – an unspoken acknowledgment that came with age. The season came with its own set of complications, that was for sure.

"Well, I hope you enjoy it." She hooked the loose curl back behind her ear and smiled again. "And I hope you enjoy the shortbread."

"I'm sure I will."

Jim picked up the shortbread, still warm from the oven, and realised that he hadn't asked her name.

3

SARAH

"Someone's sitting in my chair." Dolina folded her arms and hefted her bosom in a way that always made Sarah giggle. The snow that had fallen two days before not only showed no signs of melting but was being added to by another fall which had started mid-morning. For the third day in a row the handsome American had come in, settling himself down in the corner table by the window, writing in his notebook and ordering coffee – always black – and then something to eat with a second cup. Today it was one of her chocolate-dipped gingerbread cookies, which he broke in half with long fingers, gazing absently out of the window.

"You sound like one of the three bears," Sarah said, laughing. She waved goodbye to the couple who were heading out into the snowy street. "Look, the table by the other window is free now, Greta and Jim are just leaving."

It was mid-afternoon, and after another busy morning the rush had settled down. Three of the six tables were empty, but not Dolina's favourite spot, which had been snagged once again by the man.

Dolina pursed her lips. "Well, it'll have to do. I like that seat because it has a good view."

Sarah smiled to herself. She'd suspected that he'd chosen it for that very reason. In the little bay window, you could look out onto the snow-covered harbour, watching the occasional boat come in, and the comings and goings from the vet, the supermarket, the newly re-opened bookshop on the corner, and of course the hair salon. Sally, the owner, had told her earlier that she was rushed off her feet with last-minute appointments.

Sarah had glanced at her reflection in the mirror, vaguely conscious that it had been far too long since she'd had more than a quick trim. Unlike the other residents of Applemore, though, she didn't have any reason to get herself done up for Christmas.

"You like that seat," teased Chloe, pouring water into a teapot, "because you can see down the street and watch what's going on."

Dolina opened her mouth and then closed it again. "Fair enough," she admitted, with a chuckle. "Someone's got to keep an eye out."

"You're like the fifth emergency service." Chloe put the pot and a cup and saucer onto a tray.

Sarah groaned as Mariah Carey started up again and flicked the button on the radio, switching it over to Classic FM. The Carol of the Bells filled the room and the American looked up for a moment, catching her eye and raising a brow in acknowledgment.

"If I didn't have my ear to the ground, you'd never have known that Donald Robertson was looking for a new tenant for his cottage," Dolina said, waggling a finger.

Chloe tipped her head. "You've got a point. And now I get to cook my first ever Christmas dinner."

"I bet Alex can't wait." Dolina peered at the trays of cookies. "I'll have a couple of shortbreads as well, one to eat now and one in a wee bag, please. So, are you all organised for the big day?" She looked from Sarah to Chloe, eyebrows raised.

"I need to go to the Farm Shop later and collect the turkey. You sure you don't mind me going early?"

Sarah shook her head. "I can close up."

"It's just a big chicken, after all," Chloe said, for the twentieth time that week. "How hard can it be?"

"Not hard at all," Dolina reassured her, reaching over and putting a hand on her arm. "It's like falling off a log."

Chloe's eyes widened in mock horror.

"You'll be fine," Sarah said firmly. "And if you're not, it'll be something to laugh about."

"Unless we both die of food poisoning."

Sarah flicked her with a tea towel, making Dolina laugh.

"Bugger off to the Farm Shop now and get the turkey before I murder you myself."

"You sure?" Chloe's eyes flicked towards the door. She'd been antsy all morning.

"Never surer," growled Sarah. "I'll be fine."

Ten minutes later the café was almost empty. The only two tables left were Dolina and the American, who was gazing out of the window, tapping his pen on his chin, lost in thought.

"Ahem."

Dolina cleared her throat in a way that filled the room. Sarah knew what was coming next, and folded her arms, looking across the room with her lips pressed together to stop herself from laughing out loud.

"So," Dolina continued into the air, "I hear you're from the United States of America."

The man looked up, glancing around the room in surprise. He'd clearly been so lost in thought that he hadn't even noticed the café emptying out as he worked.

"I am, yes."

"Very nice." Dolina raised her chin and shifted her chair slightly so she could survey him more clearly. "And you're here for a wee holiday?"

"He's doing research," Sarah said with what she hoped was a warning tone.

"I am," he said, standing up and crossing the room in two long strides. He extended a hand and Dolina, eyes wide, shook it. "Jim Fletcher. Pleased to meet you."

"Dolina Allen," she said, looking sideways at Sarah. "Very nice to meet you, too."

"Would you mind if I asked you a few questions?"

Sarah lifted her hand to her mouth to stop herself from laughing, but a snort escaped from her nose, and she had to duck down behind the counter, pretending to pick up a Tupperware container. She stood up a second later, plastic tub in hand and lips pressed together.

Dolina was motioning to him to take a seat. "Of course not," she said, pulling her chair back slightly so she knocked against the wall. "Be my guest."

"Thank you so much." He sat down at the table, pulling his ever-present notebook out of his pocket. "I wanted to ask you a little about Applemore."

He met Sarah's eyes and for a second, she thought she caught the ghost of a wink.

Heat rose in her cheeks and she turned around, busying herself by wiping down the countertop and trying to ignore the heat rising in her cheeks. She was far too old to be having her head turned by a random tourist passing through Applemore – even if he was tall and good looking, with crinkles at the corners of his dark brown eyes. They, along with the wink, suggested that despite his serious demeanour there was a person in there who appreciated a joke.

"I think we're going to be needing some more tea."

Dolina was settling in, folding her arms and leaning forward on the table as if she was being interviewed for a tv show.

"Coming right up."

The snow outside seemed to underline the quiet in the almost empty café. Sarah filled the teapot and placed the cups and saucers onto the tray, trying very hard not to listen in to their conversation. With Chloe gone, she'd switched off the Christmas music in favour of some peace and quiet, so it was hard not to eavesdrop.

"Well," Dolina said as she approached the table, "Applemore ten years ago was a very different place. Those railings out there?" She waved an arm in the direction of the harbour, "They were rusting away. We'd one little shop and not to speak ill of the dead but it's no bad thing that it was replaced with the mini market. Half the things on the shelves had been there since I was a lassie, and that's no' yesterday."

Sarah, standing behind Dolina, was right in Jim's eyeline. She raised her brows as he looked up at her, knowing that Dolina was angling for a compliment.

"Oh, nonsense," he said, in his deep voice, holding Sarah's gaze for a moment. A smile was just tugging the corners of his mouth. "I'm sure it was just a few years ago."

Dolina chuckled happily. "Oh, get away with you."

Sarah shook her head, smiling to herself, and was heading back towards the kitchen when Dolina called to her.

"How long is it since they opened the Farm Shop up at Applemore House?"

She put the tea-towel she was holding over her shoulder and frowned for a moment, scrunching up her face as she thought. "Four years? Five?"

"And you think that made a difference?" Jim scribbled a note down on his pad and then stood up unexpectedly, stepping towards her with his hand extended. "I am so sorry. Please forgive my manners, or lack of them. I haven't introduced myself to you and I'm quizzing your customers. I'm Jim."

"Sarah." His handshake was firm, his hand warm as it clasped hers for a moment. "I did hear your name already," she added, "when you introduced yourself to Dolina."

"Sarah." He smiled at her and the crinkles around his eyes deepened. "You did, yes. But it's nice to know your name."

"Of course, the café here in the village has given the place a wee boost, as well." Dolina was on a roll now. "There's the coffeeshop up at the big house, but it's not much use unless you can drive. So Sarah and Evelyn made a real difference when they opened this place."

Sarah fiddled with the knot at her apron waistband, looking down for a moment.

"Evelyn was one of my best pals," Dolina carried on, "and it had always been her dream to open a little café here in the village. And to do it with her daughter—well—"

Dolina lifted the lid of the teapot and looked inside for a moment before she looked up again with damp eyes. "It was nice that she got to see her dream come true."

Jim cleared his throat, and Dolina gave a little sniff. Sarah pulled the end of the apron tie a little too hard and the knot came undone in her hands, so she had to tie it back up as she spoke.

"My mother died three months after the café opened," she explained. "We've been open three years this week."

"And you've done her proud," said Dolina, reaching around to squeeze her on the arm.

Jim didn't say anything, but his brows lifted slightly in query, as if he was silently asking if she was okay. She found herself nodding in response.

"I think a place like this can be the real heart of a community. It certainly seems to be from what I've seen over the last couple of days."

"Oh, there's a lot more than this," Sarah said, watching as Dolina poured the tea without waiting to ask how Jim took his, or even if he wanted any. "We have lots of different community things going on – there's a little library out at the lighthouse, and we have the community cupboard which is a sort of foods and goods exchange."

Jim, who'd been handed a cup of very strong milky tea, nodded slowly. "This is exactly the sort of thing I'm interested in hearing about. And tourists?"

"*Och*, we've got tourists coming out of our ears."

"Excuse me," Sarah said, reluctant to leave but aware that she needed to get the place cleared up before closing. "I must get tidied up."

"Of course."

Fifteen minutes or so had passed, by which time Sarah had cleared the tables, wiping down the red and white gingham covers and straightening all the chairs so the café was ready for the next morning. Chloe had dashed in and out to pick up a bag she'd forgotten, looking wild-eyed and pink in the face with the car parked outside, the engine still running.

Sarah was just wiping off the board to write up tomorrow's specials when Dolina jumped up from her chair with a shriek of surprise.

"Oh heavens," she said, pulling on her coat. "I need to run. Jenny's got stuck up at the Farm Shop and the little ones are waiting round the corner at the after-school club."

Jim looked on, his brows lifting in concern.

"Sorry, Sarah," she said, hooking her bag over her shoulder and checking her watch again. "Can I run back in with the money in the morning?"

"No need," said Jim, standing up. "It's on me. It's the least I can do to thank you for your help."

"Are you sure?" Dolina beamed as she zipped up her coat and wound a purple scarf around her neck. "That's awfully kind of you."

"I am certain."

It sounded really nice in his accent. Sarah watched as Dolina hurtled out of the door and sped off in the direction of the little primary school around the corner. After a moment she remembered that she was now standing alone in the café with only a handsome American for company, and she suddenly felt oddly shy.

"I'm sorry," he said, following her over to the counter. "I feel I've taken up your afternoon. It says on the sign you close at three thirty."

"We usually do," Sarah pulled the bib of her apron. "Because we're up so early baking, it's a really long day."

"Do you make all this yourself?" He cast a look along the counter.

"We do. I made a decision after... when my mum died, I realised that we were overstretching ourselves. I wanted to make the place somewhere people could get a coffee and something to eat, but with the hotel and the farm shop as well, I didn't want to make it too fancy."

"So, you stick to the tried and tested favourites."

"Pretty much. In the winter – especially at Christmas – it's the same things everyone wants. Gingerbread, cookies, some shortbread, and a cup of tea. Chloe and I take it in turns to get up and do the baking."

"Hard work." He rested a hand on the counter, and she glanced down at it, noticing that he was wearing a wedding ring. Of course he was married.

"It keeps me out of mischief." Sarah gave a wry smile.

"And do you find yourself in mischief – as a rule?"

"Hardly. It's pretty hard to get up to anything in a village like Applemore. Everyone knows everyone's business, and there's never anything going on."

"That's the direct opposite of what I've just been hearing from Dolina." He laughed. "She led me to believe Applemore was a hotbed of intrigue."

"Dolina would find gossip if you left her alone in the desert." Sarah shook her head with a fond laugh. "I've known her all my life, and she's always had an unerring ability to find out what everyone is up to."

"So, your opportunities for misbehaviour have been curtailed by village gossips."

"Something like that." She leaned back on the counter and crossed her legs at the ankle, looking at him with interest. "So, are you heading back to the USA for Christmas?"

Jim shook his head. "No, I'm here for the whole of the

holidays. I thought it would be a good chance to see Applemore, and it looks like I chose well. It's beautiful out there."

They both looked out of the window at the snowy street, where parents and their children were returning, hand-in-hand, from the school pick-up, dressed in colourful winter coats and throwing snowballs over the harbour railing. It looked like a picture postcard.

"You chose a good year. We hardly ever get snow here."

"Where I come from, there's snow pretty much all winter."

"And your family," Sarah said, her curiosity getting the better of her, "do they not mind you spending Christmas so far away?"

Jim shook his head with a half-smile. "My daughter is currently working in Madagascar – she's an ornithologist."

The question was hanging in the air.

"My wife died five years ago."

"Oh, I'm so sorry." Sarah put a hand to her mouth. "I'm—I shouldn't have asked."

He shook his head. "Not at all. I'm—well, I wouldn't say it's something you get over, but I guess you'd say I've come to terms with it. I was lucky to be married for twenty-five years. Lots of people don't get that."

She picked up a tea towel from the counter and folded it in half, smoothing it out with her hand before folding it once again and looking up. "No, they don't."

"You're not married?"

It was his turn to look at her hand.

"No, I'm not. It just—well, for one reason and another. Here I am."

"Well, it's a beautiful part of the world to live."

"It really is. Although people often miss the best parts.

They tend to breeze in and out – we're on the North Coast 500 route, so a lot of the time you get the feeling they're ticking us off on their list before they move on to the next spot."

If she didn't stop folding the tea towel it was going to be the size of a postage stamp. She slid it out of reach as he reached into his pocket, bringing out a dark brown leather wallet.

"Do you have any recommendations?"

Sarah frowned in thought. "There's a beautiful beach walk out beyond the Applemore Farm Shop. It's officially private land, but the Fraser family have never objected to people walking there. I used to take my dog all the time."

"Oh, a dog person." He pulled out his credit card and waited while she tapped on the screen of the cash register. "I thought I liked you."

Now her cheeks were definitely going pink. "I had a labrador, Charlie," she said, passing over the payment unit.

"The only trouble with dogs is they don't live as long as us," he said as the machine bleeped. He shook his head as she offered a receipt. "Did you lose him recently?"

"Oh, Charlie was a she." She smiled at the thought of Charlie's chocolate-drop eyes and lugubrious expression. "My nephew named her. He was so disappointed that she wasn't a boy that we let him go along with it. He was desperate for a brother at the time."

"And now?"

"Oh, now he's seventeen and getting ready for art school."

"And he got over the disappointment in the end?" His eyes twinkled as they met hers.

Sarah nodded, laughing. "I think he's getting there, yes."

"Glad to hear it." He put his wallet back in his pocket and

picked up a leaflet about the Christmas carol concert. "Would you recommend this?"

"If it carries on snowing, I think you'll be guaranteed a full turnout. Is it the town you're interested in, or the people?"

"You can't have one without the other." He folded the leaflet in half and put it in the back pocket of his jeans. "I guess it'll be a good chance to see how the place ticks."

"And you're analysing a lot of Scottish villages?"

"A few. Applemore's the last one on my list, and then I'm back to New England to take a look at a couple of places in Maine. There's a little town called Bangor. I've got some old friends up there so I'm going to pay them a visit."

"It sounds like an interesting job. Are you a professor?"

"I am." He pushed a hand through his hair, ducking his head for a moment. "I'm on sabbatical for now, but once I've done this study I'll be back to teaching."

"In New England," Sarah sighed wistfully. "I've always wanted to go there. It looks so beautiful."

She'd watched the videos on Instagram of cute little painted houses set against the backdrop of red-leaved trees in the fall, and couples in warm hats cosied up with cups of hot apple cider. Back when she was younger, she'd dreamed of travelling, but somehow…

"Oh, it is." Jim smiled and glanced outside as two teenagers ran past the window, shouting and laughing with the unmistakable delight that came with the end of the school term. "I'm sure there are plenty of New Englanders who'd love to visit Applemore, mind you."

"We get quite a few Americans, you're right." She raised her brows without thinking, remembering the family of six from California who'd turned up when they were closing and complained bitterly that she didn't have any green juice. "Just like the people of Applemore, they're generally nice."

His mouth twisted in a half-smile. "Sounds like there's a story in there."

"Let's just say that if you're a gluten free family, a bakery cafe is probably not the best place to visit."

He chuckled and shook his head.

"Well, there's hope for me. I'll be in again tomorrow, and I'm very much looking forward to as much gluten as you have to offer."

He raised his hand in a wave as he turned to leave, buttoning his grey wool coat with one hand.

"If you want," Sarah found herself saying, surprising herself, "I'm off tomorrow afternoon if you'd like someone to show you some of the spots you might miss otherwise."

"I'd love that." Jim turned to look at her with a broad smile. "That would be really great."

"Okay. I'm—um, I-I'll be done by mid-day."

"Perfect. I was planning to take a walk round the village in the morning, but I'll come by at ten thirty, have some of your excellent coffee waiting, and we can head off as soon as you're ready."

"Great."

"I'll look forward to it."

She watched as he strode over to the door, pausing with his hand on the doorframe for a second as he adjusted his scarf. The fairy lights twinkled in the window, warm against grey light of a midwinter afternoon.

"Thanks, Sarah."

"Oh," she said, biting her lip for a moment as she felt heat rising in her cheeks. It was ridiculous. "You're welcome."

4

JIM

A pink-haired girl was pinning up some more decorations to the already-festive entrance to the Applemore Hotel as Jim paused for a moment to read a notice on the board by the front desk.

"Did you enjoy the quiz last night?" She turned to look at him, a roll of tape in one hand and a swag of gold tinsel in the other.

"I did." He smiled. "I had no idea that it would be so competitive."

"Oh, it's fierce all year round but the Christmas quiz is another level." She cocked her head and looked at the decoration she'd just hung, then searched for the end of the tape as she carried on talking. "D'you think it'll end up in your book?"

He chuckled. "It's not a book, I'm afraid. Just some research for a study I'm doing."

"There goes my chance of fame." She pouted. "But Applemore's going to get a good report?"

"Oh, the very best." He pulled on his gloves, glancing up

at the clock above the desk. It was ten thirty, and he'd told Sarah he'd be there at the café. Somehow it mattered that he wasn't late. "I'm very impressed with the place so far. And I'm off on a walk today to find out a little more. I intend to take in the whole Applemore experience."

"You need to go up to the Farm Shop and see the market today, then. They've got Santa coming after lunch." She did a little dance of excitement. "I love Christmas, don't you?"

Jim nodded, heading for the door. "Absolutely." He raised a hand in farewell. "Have a good day."

It seemed that the holiday season was sending everyone in the village slightly crazy. Last night's quiz had been uproarious, the hotel bar packed with guests and locals. He'd wandered through after a quiet meal for a dram of whisky by the fire to find the place as crazy as Times Square at New Years. It was standing room only at the bar, and groups of people were crammed around close-packed tables. He'd been co-opted for one of the teams by Harry, the hotel owner, who'd said that if he wanted the real Applemore experience he couldn't miss out.

The real Applemore experience had involved several more drams of malt whisky, as well as some good beer brewed by one of his team-mates called Lachlan, who ran the local brewery. He'd been surprised to discover several hours into the evening that the laid back, easy-going guy with a scruff of dark beard and a hole in the elbow of his sweater was the Laird of Applemore.

"Ah, that's a stroke of luck. I hoped I'd bump into you again."

He walked out of the door slap bang into Dolina, who was wearing a red knitted hat with reindeer antlers sticking out of either side and a hopeful expression.

"Dolina, hello."

"How's your head after last night?"

He laughed and shook his head. "Not bad at all. I've had a full Scottish breakfast and a pot of tea and I'm just on my way to have a coffee and do some work."

She put a hand on his arm, holding him in place. "Yes, that's what I wanted to talk to you about. I had to rush off and I hadn't finished filling you in on everything."

She paused for a moment as a dark-haired woman rushed past with her arms full of packages.

"Morning, Sophie. How's it going?"

"Good thanks Dolina, just on my way to the post office. Can't stop, I don't want to miss the post!" She set off at a jog, her dark ponytail swinging.

"That's one of our vets," Dolina said, raising a finger. "She's no' long in the village, herself. And her partner Ben is an artist. He makes these big sculpture things out of bits of driftwood. He said I had a talent for art, you know."

Jim smiled and pushed back his coat sleeve, checking his watch. Almost ten forty.

"I—" he began.

"Of course, the art classes and the Flower Farm have made a difference. You'll be wanting to put that in your book."

He opened his mouth to explain once again that he wasn't writing a book, then closed it again and nodded once.

"And of course there's the gastro pub in the hotel there, that's made a difference especially now they've got one of those Mitchell stars."

"A Mitchell star?"

"For the cooking."

"Ah, of course." He felt his brows raising slightly.

"And then there's Midsummer House where they do respite care, that put us on the map as well. And Charlotte Fraser's holiday cottages." She paused to draw breath, hand raised as she counted each of Applemore's benefits on a finger. "And of course there's the—"

Jim thought quickly. "Do you know, Dolina, this is great information."

She beamed at him. "Glad to hear it. I'm only just getting started."

It was his turn to raise a finger. "May I stop you for one moment?"

"Of course." Her breath clouded in the cold air.

"I have some work to do today, but perhaps I could buy you a coffee" – he watched as her mouth opened to protest and corrected himself midsentence – "sorry, a pot of tea, and I can take this all down with my notebook in hand."

Dolina took a step back, looking pleased. "A meeting?"

"Absolutely. It would be my pleasure. Tomorrow afternoon?"

"I'll see if I can fit it in." She chuckled at her own joke. "I've got a busy schedule, you know."

"How about two thirty?"

"I'll see you at the café."

Laughing to himself, he hurried along the main street towards the café. There had been another fall of snow overnight, and the sea was an inky dark blue against the white of the harbour. The clouds that gathered above were a strange pinkish grey, and the air was crisp and cold, reminding him of New England.

He pushed open the door to the café and found himself smiling broadly at Sarah, who looked up from the counter, where she was talking to a tiny woman with a head of dark curls.

"Hi," he mouthed, lifting a hand in greeting. Three of the tables were already taken, but his spot by the window had clearly just been vacated. He tucked himself in, putting the empty cups and saucers to one side, and flipped open his MacBook.

"Hello," Sarah said a few minutes later, holding a cloth in one hand and a wooden tray in the other. "Let me take these away for you."

She was wearing a red-and-white striped T-shirt under her apron, her hair tied back in a loose bun at the nape of her neck. One dark curl had come loose and hung down to the curve of her collarbone, and there was a smudge of flour on her cheek.

"I was caught by Dolina," he found himself explaining.

"Oh," Sarah said, her face lifting in a smile. "I wondered if you'd maybe—"

"Decided against our trip this afternoon? No way. I've been looking forward to it."

She bit her lip then, ducking her head as her cheeks flushed a pretty pink. So, she had noticed his tardiness.

"I'm glad. My friend Anna – she's the girl I was talking to when you came in – is going to do the delivery after we close."

"Delivery?"

"Yes," she said, turning as a voice called her name. "I'll explain it all when I'm done here. What can I get you? The usual?"

Something in his chest warmed at the words and he nodded. "Yes, please. And one of your famous gingerbread cookies would be great."

"Coming," she said, calling to her assistant who was motioning from the door behind the counter. "I'll get that for you in just a moment."

He ran a hand across his jaw, hiding the smile he couldn't seem to stop from spreading across his face as he watched her walking back across the café and slipping through the doorway into the kitchen.

A few moments later a freckled girl with bright ginger hair interrupted his train of thought as she crashed a tray down on the table beside his computer.

"Ooh, sorry," she said with a giggle. "I misjudged that."

"Not a problem," he said, steadying the coffee cup with a cautious hand. Sarah looked over from the counter where she was serving a sturdy looking woman with steely-grey hair. He raised his brows in acknowledgment.

"Can I get you anything else?"

"No, that's perfect, thank you," he said, picking up the gingerbread. It was shaped like a Christmas tree with finely piped white icing decorating each pointed branch, and when he snapped off a piece, he discovered it was melt in the mouth delicious.

Sarah's workmate was wearing a halo of purple tinsel around her head and dancing to the music on the radio. As he worked the café filled up, every table buzzing with a palpable sense of excitement.

Look what I saw today!

He picked up his phone with the surge of love he always felt when a message from Laurel appeared. A moment later an image of his daughter holding some sort of exotic bird appeared. She looked tan and happy, her dark hair tied back from her face in a plait that hung down her shoulder in the same way that her mother's had when they first met.

> Beautiful!

> Me or the bird?

> You know I'm a sucker for a colorful beak. How's it going over there in sunny Madagascar?

> Amazing. Pretty weird to think that it's snowing right now in Silverford.

> We've got snow right here in Scotland

He snapped a photograph through the window and hit send. A moment or two later Laurel's reply appeared.

> Does it feel weird being there?

> A little. There?

> Sorta. It's an adventure. Mom said we should have lots of them.

> She did, little one, you're right. She'd be so proud of you.

> And you, Dad. I love you!

> Love you too, little one.

> I'll message you tonight. Let me know how your exploring goes ••

The eyeball emoji she sent made him laugh out loud in the middle of the café, and the women at the table looked at him for a second – both turning their heads in surprise before they continued with their conversation.

He wasn't sure why he'd mentioned Sarah to his daughter the day before. He had travelled all over Scotland for the last six weeks, meeting people and seeing places, finding his way around the small towns that had grown and thrived in a challenging economy. And yet, for some reason, he'd found himself telling her that the kind-hearted woman from the café had offered to show him around in her free time.

He'd spoken to plenty people. But there was something about her that he was drawn to – a strange sense that Laurel would like her, somehow. And that Meg would have, too. Maybe that was all it was.

He shook his head and returned to his notebook, flipping over the pages he'd written the day before. He had a couple of hours to type them up to the accompaniment of the noise and bustle of the café, and the off-key singing of Sarah's co-worker behind the counter.

"I'll be with you in just a moment," Sarah said as she wiped the table beside him. "Just need to make myself a bit less floury."

He looked up at her for a moment and smiled. She looked good just as she was.

"Ready?" she said a few moments later, emerging from the back kitchen. She was holding a thick green coat in her arms.

"Thank you very much," he said, paying the bill.

"No problem at all," said Sarah's workmate, giving her a sideways look that was clearly supposed to be subtle. "Have a good walk."

"Thanks, Chloe," said Sarah, flashing her a direct, wide-eyed look. He didn't miss that, either.

"I'll call you later about the turkey."

Sarah laughed and rolled her eyes. "Let's go."

She had her car keys in hand and jingled them as they stepped out into the pale light. In the harbour a little boat was just heading out to sea, a flock of gulls wheeling overhead in the hope of fish.

"I thought we'd take a walk first, and then perhaps we could pop by the Farm Shop, and you can take a look – if you haven't been there already?"

Jim shook his head. "No, I thought I'd wait and have the guided tour. It's much nicer to visit with someone than alone."

Sarah opened the car doors and motioned for him to climb into her little Ford Focus.

"Sorry," she said as he was fastening his belt. "This must seem tiny compared to your big American cars."

"I hired a little one at the airport in Glasgow, and I've made it all the way across the Scottish Highlands so far without complaints."

"Oh yes, I forgot about that." She crunched the gears and laughed. "Sorry, my brother always teases me about my driving. I think I've got performance anxiety."

"It's nice to be driven. It means I can take notes if I need to."

They headed out of the village, past a row of low, white-washed cottages.

"Those are known as the fisherman's cottages, but a lot of them are holiday lets now." Sarah pointed to one with pretty planters full of flowers on the window ledges. "That one belongs to my old schoolteacher. She's retired now."

"It's cute."

They drove up and up, past spindly black hedges blanketed with snow.

"It's really unusual to have snow for more than a day here in Applemore. You must've brought it with you."

"Sorry about that."

She shook her head, her hair – now loosed from its knot and hanging around her shoulders – flying as she laughed. "Oh no, don't apologise. It's usually grey and raining at this time of year, so this is really lovely. Is it snowy with you every Christmas?"

"Pretty much without exception. And cold, too. Twenty, thirty below most winters."

She glanced over at him, brows knitted in thought.

"Oh sorry," he said a moment later. "I forget we're divided by a common language. Well below zero, even in your measurement."

"Wow, that really is cold. That's amazing."

He lifted his gloves. "Hence coming prepared."

"It's lucky you did." They turned off the road, passing a painted sign which indicated they were en-route to Applemore Farm Shop, and a lot more besides.

"A brewery, an outdoor adventure centre, a shop..." he said aloud.

"And the arts centre, another bakery, and the Flower Farm." Sarah pulled the car to a halt in a gap by a wooden gate. "This is us."

5

SARAH

She grimaced as she opened the car door. Why on earth did she just say, "us" as if they were a *we*.

Jim didn't seem to have noticed. Pulling his woollen hat on, he stood by the car with an arm resting on the roof as she wrapped a scarf around her neck and fastened her coat.

"Sorry, I should have done all this before we left."

"Don't worry. I'm enjoying the scenery."

He looked at her for a moment and then looked away, his gaze taking in the snow-covered fields that led down the path towards the beach. The trail had been resurfaced a while back with woodchips supplied by the forestry, and there was still a pile of leftover chips waiting by the gate.

"Oh, there's the forestry, as well." She pocketed her car keys and pulled on a pair of red gloves, looking at her reflection in the car window. She looked like a Christmas gnome in her red hat, but it was far too cold to go out without it. *Not,* she reminded herself firmly, *that it mattered what she looked like.* She was taking a visitor for a walk out of the kindness of her heart, and nothing more.

He opened the wooden gate and waited as she walked through before closing the metal latch.

"I took a walk over to the Lighthouse to see the visitor centre yesterday. It's pretty impressive."

"Did you climb up to the top?"

"Of course. I couldn't come all this way and look at it from ground level." He smiled, looking at her for a moment. "And I had a peek at the Lighthouse Library, too. We have a little Free Library like that back home in Silverford."

"It's another one of those things that seemed to set the village alight. It's funny, but it's been like a snowball effect." Sarah ran a hand along the hedge as they walked, tracing the top of the layer of white that covered the bare branches. She scooped up a handful and pressed it into a ball, feeling the squeaky crunch of it against the wool of her glove.

"That seems to be the secret with the small towns I've seen that are thriving." Jim stepped sideways to allow her to go ahead as the path narrowed for a moment. "The decline is so gradual that people don't even notice. One little store closes, then people start heading elsewhere to pick up their groceries. Then when they're out of town they figure they might as well stop for a cup of coffee, and then the café in the village starts to suffer."

"Especially in the current financial climate." Sarah nodded with feeling. "People don't have the disposable income they once had."

"Precisely. And then of course it seems to work the other way. Look at Applemore."

She turned to look at him for a moment, watching as he thought for a moment. *He was*, she thought, *a proper grown up*. And not in a bad way. He looked like the sort of man who would be responsible for things.

"We've been lucky," she admitted. "It all started, really, when Lachlan inherited the estate. He nearly sold it at first. I think he felt guilty that he was entitled to everything and his sisters weren't."

"Ah, yes. The blessing and the curse of the British aristocracy," Jim laughed, doing an impressively accurate impression of an upper-class Englishman.

"Funny to think of Lachlan as aristocracy. He's very down to earth."

"I agree."

"You met him?"

"At the hotel quiz last night, funnily enough. I was asked to make up the numbers on the team."

"Oh, I love that," she smiled again. "If you want to get an idea of what Applemore is like, I'd say that the quiz is a pretty good insight. Did you get the chance to ask many questions?"

He grinned, dimples deepening on his cheeks. "Unfortunately, not. It was a little too rowdy, and there was a lot of malt whisky being drunk, not to mention Lachlan's own beer."

"Maybe you'll see him when we go up to the Farm Shop. It's his sister, Polly, who runs it. There are usually several Frasers floating around the estate – his other sister, Beth, runs the Flower Farm up here."

"Yes, I was reading about it this morning. Back to your snowball effect."

Sarah bit her lip and nodded, remembering that she was there to impart information. "Yes, so the estate was inherited by Lachlan, and the Flower Farm just grew—"

"As one might expect," he teased, eyes crinkling,

"Well yes." Sarah laughed again. "And then the Farm

Shop happened, and then Tom and Gavin opened the coffeeshop, and Matt started the bakery, and—"

"And then you opened the café?"

"I did. Well, we did." They'd almost reached the beach now, winding down between the two ploughed fields towards the rocks. "It's funny, if you'd told me ten years ago I'd have been doing this, I'd have thought you were insane."

"What were you doing ten years ago?"

A gust of wind blew her scarf forwards and she caught it, tossing it back over her shoulder.

"I was working as an estate agent in the town nearby." It was hard to imagine she'd spent twenty years driving all over their patch of the Highlands, showing off houses and farms to prospective buyers and crossing her fingers in the hope of a good month of commission.

"You were?" He paused for a moment, turning to look at her. "That seems like a strange jump. But all that time you were dreaming of running your own little bakery café?"

She shook her head, laughing. "Far from it."

"But your cookies are out of this world."

"Baking is a science, really. It's just a case of measuring and timing."

"I think you're doing yourself a disservice. I've tried a lot of cookies on my travels, and yours are by far the best."

Embarrassed, Sarah pulled at the hem of her coat sleeve, tugging it down over her glove. When she looked up, Jim was still looking at her.

"I believe in giving compliments where they're due."

In his accent it made her go a bit funny at the knees.

"In that case, thank you," she said, hooking a strand of hair back behind her ear and adjusting her woolly hat. "So yes, to go back to what you were saying, no, it wasn't really *my* dream."

His voice was gentle. "But it was your mum's."

Something in the kindness of his tone made her eyes prickle for a moment and she pressed her lips together as she nodded, wordlessly.

"I'm sorry, I didn't mean to cause upset."

"Not at all." She shook her head. "It's funny how grief works, isn't it? You think you're fine then someone plays a song in the supermarket when you're buying soup and you're crying."

He gave a huff of laughter. "That is a pretty good summary, yeah."

"Oh, I'm sorry."

"No, please don't apologise. Meg used to say, 'you're going to have a lot of life left without me in it, so you better go enjoy it'."

"Is that why you're here?" She rubbed her forehead under her hat.

"With you?" He raised his eyebrows, a wry smile tugging at his lips.

"Oh," she covered her face with her hands, realising what she'd said, "I meant in Scotland."

"I know what you meant." Jim gave a warm laugh. "Yes and no."

They were at the beach now, and the water lapped gently against the white sand. The snow followed a neat line from the morning's tide, edged with a dark line of seaweed and driftwood.

"Our daughter, Laurel, messaged me earlier from *her* research trip. It's the first Christmas we've spent apart, so I guess we're both finding our way."

"Christmas is complicated, isn't it? All those expectations to have fun concentrated into one day." She thought of Chloe, and her obsession with getting the turkey just right. She'd caught her earlier, comparing two printed recipes and muttering about brining the thing in a bucket for twenty-four hours beforehand.

"It's a lot of pressure. Turns out it's fun to do something different. Who knew I'd be walking on a Highland beach the day before Christmas Eve." He bent to pick up a black pebble, smoothed flat by countless tides.

"It's been ages since I was here, too." It was ridiculous really to live in such a pretty place and not take advantage of it.

"Because you lost your dog?" He looked at her for a moment. "It must feel strange to be here without her."

"It does. But I was just thinking that sometimes it takes seeing a place through someone else's eyes to realise what you take for granted."

The strange sky was deepening in colour, the clouds threatening yet more snow. As they stood, the first flakes started to fall, dancing through the air. Each one was tiny – a little speck of glitter.

Jim shaded his eyes, looking out at the distant shapes of the islands. "I think you're right. I wonder what you'd see if you visited New England."

Sarah's stomach flipped over at the thought, and she curled her gloved hands into fists, taking a long breath in at the thought of something she'd put aside – the idea of travel and escape, seeing more of the world, maybe even—

"Perhaps one day you can see for yourself." Jim reached out, brushing the snow from her shoulders.

She pulled in a breath in surprise at his touch.

"Maybe one day."

There was a moment of silence and then she gathered herself, clearing her throat and turning back towards the path.

"Anyway, I really ought to show you the Farm Shop before the weather turns. It looks like we might be in for even more snow. It's unbelievable."

She could hear her voice sounding higher and brighter than normal, and all the way back to the car she kept up a string of chatter about the various businesses that had opened in the village, and what a difference the improvement society had made, and how lovely it was to have a chance to tell someone all about Applemore.

"Hopefully I've given you enough information for you to give us a good report," she said brightly, as she opened the car doors.

"I couldn't ask for more." Jim smiled, folding his long legs into the passenger seat beside her. "Now perhaps you'll let me buy you something to eat as a thank you. I hear your rival does a pretty good lunch."

Sarah laughed as she turned the keys. "That sounds like a deal."

6

JIM

If he hadn't done his research The Applemore Farm Shop would have come as a surprise. From the down-home name, you'd be expecting a cute little farm stall, with some home-made produce, and maybe a few baked items. But the rows of cars lining the road, and the packed car park out back told another story altogether. They pulled up beside a glossy Range Rover and Sarah turned off the engine, turning to look at him with her brows raised.

"Brace yourself," she said with a laugh. "I think it might be a little bit busy in here."

"I'll be taking notes." He released his belt and climbed out. The snow was whirling down in ever-thickening flakes, giving the parked cars a festive sugar dusting. A young couple walked by, laughing as they dragged a huge Christmas tree covered in red netting and tried to lift it onto the roof of their tiny car.

"Do you want a hand with that?" he called across and the girl turned to him, wiping tears of laughter from her eyes.

"Yes please, if you don't mind."

He took one end and together they hefted it into place, holding it as they passed straps through the car window opening and tied it down.

"Reminds me of back home," he said to Sarah as they started walking down towards the farm buildings. "We used to go buy a tree from the Christmas tree farm every winter."

Ahead of them stood a collection of solid, white-washed buildings. Their grey slate roofs were dusted with snow, and smoke rose from a chimney, wafting a scent of wood fires into the air.

"Do you know, I haven't even got a tree this year. Is that a terrible confession?" Sarah turned to him as she pulled off her hat and shook out her hair, running a hand through it. A snowflake landed on her dark lashes, and she swiped it away, smiling. "I've been so busy with the café, and it just sort of passed by."

"First year I haven't had one since college." He lifted a shoulder in a shrug. "So, I guess we can be grinches together."

"I won't tell if you don't." Her nose crinkled as she shot him a conspiratorial grin.

And then they turned the corner into the courtyard where Christmas definitely hadn't been passed by. A huge pine tree was decorated with thousands of sparkling white fairy lights, and the air was rich with the smell of cinnamon and hot mulled wine emanating from a silver Airstream caravan which was parked by the side of a renovated barn. Huge windows were hung with children's cut-out snowflakes and the place was thronging with noise and bustle. Christmas music was playing through the speakers, and the wooden benches that lined the tables were crammed with people laughing and chatting, surrounded by piles of bags of shopping and parcels.

"Okay, this is pretty impressive."

"Yeah, from one little shop selling local fruit and vegetables." Sarah nodded hello to an older man in a woollen cap, his collar turned up against the cold. "Have a good Christmas, George, if I don't see you before."

He looked at them and smiled, and Jim was very conscious that he was being given the once-over. One thing he'd learned in his studies of what made small towns tick was that they were sustained by a fuel of inside information and gossip. No doubt his visit with Sarah would be noted down and discussed that evening.

"We'll be seeing you at the carols round the tree, surely," the man chided, with a waggle of his finger. "If Greta thought you were ducking out, she'd be round to the house to pull you out from in front of that Netflix."

"I'll be there." She looked at him for a moment and he caught a glimpse of mischief in her eyes. "I'm taking Jim here, actually."

"Are you indeed?"

"Yup." He watched as she reached out, patting the older man on the arm. "Save a mulled wine for me."

"I will."

Before Jim had the chance to ask her if she'd deliberately put the cat among the pigeons they were met by another couple, trying to herd several children.

"Sarah," nodded the man, spreading his arms wide. "Good to see you. Can't stop, we're trying to get this lot back up to the house."

"That's Lachlan's brother-in-law," she explained as they made their way through the packed courtyard towards the coffee shop. "And the woman was Charlotte, his sister. It's a real family affair here."

Inside the coffee shop was stylish and modern, with metal pipework and bare brick walls hung with strings of white lights.

The man behind the counter waved enthusiastically and pointed to an empty table in the corner.

"Sit," he instructed. "I'll be over in a second."

They squeezed into the tiny space. Jim felt his knee brush against hers as he pulled in the chair and he looked up for a moment, their eyes meeting.

"Sorry."

"Don't apologise." She smiled. "It's a bit of a squash."

"I don't mind at all."

"So, this is a pretty good illustration for your research, I guess?" Sarah waved her arm in an arc, taking in the bustling coffee shop packed with customers. "Through the archway over there is the Farm Shop that started it all."

He smiled back at her, watching as she unwrapped herself from the winter layers, hanging her coat on the back of her chair and folding up the red scarf and hat that brought out the colour of her dark hair and showed off her pretty brown eyes.

The strange thing was, he didn't want to talk about research. He wanted to ask why someone as kind-hearted and well-loved by everyone in the little village of Applemore was all alone, with no plans for Christmas.

"So—" he began, but as soon as he started to speak, he was interrupted by a firm hand on his shoulder. He turned to see a grinning man, hair in dark gelled spikes and brows raised sky high, looking at him with an expectant expression.

"Hello there," the man said to Jim, while looking very

directly at Sarah. "You've taken your visitor to get a *decent* cup of coffee, I see."

"Very funny." Sarah pulled a face at him, rolling her eyes. "Jim, this is Gavin, owner of the coffee shop. Despite his terrible sense of humour, I am very fond of him."

"The feeling's mutual. Coffee?"

"Please." Sarah raised her brows.

"Black, please. And may we see the menu?"

"Sure thing." Gavin nodded. "The specials are up on the board, as well. I'll get one sent over to you in a moment. I'd love to stay and chat," he added, and Jim watched as he raised a brow at Sarah and gave her a meaningful look, "but this place is chaos today."

He blew a kiss at Sarah, then headed back over to the kitchen.

"Sorry about that," she said, laughing. "Tom and Gavin run this place, and we have a running joke about who makes the best coffee."

Jim looked at her thoughtfully, resting his chin in his hand.

"I think he'll have a hard job beating your coffee."

"I think you might be biased." Sarah's mouth curved up in a smile, the lines at the edges of her eyes crinkling.

"That's not a Scottish accent?" Jim looked over towards the counter where Gavin was already busy with his back to them, tending to the coffee machine in a cloud of steam.

"No, Gavin's from Wales. Tom's from here in Applemore. They've been running it together for years now. They've got two cute sausage dogs – they're normally over there by the fire, but I think they've probably left them back home because it's so busy at Christmas."

Their coffee arrived a couple of moments later, along with

a couple of printed paper menus. They scanned them in silence for a moment then ordered toasted sandwiches with cranberry sauce on the side. Jim listened while Sarah explained how the Farm Shop had grown year on year.

"We all work together and it's pretty harmonious, most of the time. If I need cover, I can rely on Tom and Gavin giving me a hand if they can, and with another baker up here, if I need to take time off, I can always call on Matt and Anna to supply the bread and cakes for the café."

"So, you can get time off?" He shifted sideways in his chair as a young boy of about twenty arrived with their food.

Sarah ducked her head with a half-smile.

"I can, yes."

"But you're not very good at taking it."

"Something like that. I feel responsible for making sure the café runs smoothly."

"Because of your mother's legacy?" He snapped off a crust from his toasted sandwich, the melted Brie hanging in strings. "Messy stuff, this."

She offered him a paper napkin. "Yeah, I think so. I feel a responsibility to—"

"Sarah," an urgent voice came from over his shoulder, and he turned to see a heavyset man of about thirty with close-cropped dark hair in a blue farmer's boilersuit. "Oh, am I glad to see you." The man gave an apologetic grimace, raising both hands in apology. "Sorry to interrupt your meal but I really needed to grab you when Chloe wasn't about."

Sarah dabbed at her lips. "Jim, this is Alex – Chloe's partner."

Alex pulled out the chair from the adjoining table, straddling it backwards as he sat down and leaned in, his voice low and conspiratorial. "Mind if I join you for one second?"

Jim shrugged and shook his head as Sarah glanced at him for confirmation.

"Of course not," she said with a smile.

"Hallelujah." Alex picked up a sugar sachet, jiggling it against the palm of his hand in an agitated manner.

Jim tried to suppress the irrational niggle of irritation he felt at the interruption. He was grabbing a bite to eat with someone who'd done him a favour, nothing more. So why did he feel like Alex was crashing something entirely different?

Sarah's eyes met his for a fleeting second before she shifted her body slightly, turning to Alex.

"What's up?"

"Do you want me to—" Jim began, wondering if he should excuse himself.

"Oh no," Alex shook his head, "I could use a guy's perspective."

Jim steepled his fingers, leaning in. "You could?"

"So, Chloe's doing Christmas dinner," Alex said, making Sarah groan in mock despair.

"Yes, I've had nothing but turkey talk for weeks now. She's been watching Martha Stewart re-runs and memorising Nigella Lawson's Christmas recipes like she's preparing for her university finals."

"Aye, that's what I'm worried about. She's so stressed about the dinner I don't want it to ruin the moment."

"What moment?" Sarah hooked her hair behind her ears and looked at him expectantly.

"I want to propose." Alex lowered his voice and raised a finger to his lips. "Don't say a word," he added, as Sarah's eyes widened in surprise.

"When do you think I should do it? Before the dinner or

after? During? You're good at cooking, you know timings and stuff. You know me, I'm more of a beans on toast sort of guy."

Sarah blinked hard for a moment, her face softening.

"She's going to have the turkey in mid-morning, I should think, so I would say after the presents but while you're waiting for it to cook would be perfect." She reached over, closing her hand over Alex's for a moment. "I think you could do it in the middle of the night or when she's brushing her teeth and she'd be over the moon. She's going to be so delighted. I thought you said you weren't into weddings?"

Alex shrugged, a hint of colour rising in his weather-beaten cheeks. "A man can change his mind." He looked at Jim as if seeking confirmation.

"That he can." Jim grinned. "Best of luck to you both."

"Before the dinner," Alex said, more to himself than anything. "Right. Aye. Well, I won't keep you, sorry to inter-rupt your lunch."

"Not at all." Jim stood up to shake his hand.

"Keep me posted," Sarah called, as he made his way through the packed tables, looking the closest to a bull in a China shop as anything Jim had ever seen.

Sarah looked out of the window, biting her lower lip for a moment as she watched the crowds outside.

"That's really special," Jim said as she turned back to look at him.

Sarah nodded and blinked hard one more time. "It is, isn't it?"

For a moment it felt as if they were in a space outside of the excited noise and bustle, as if the clatter of dishes and the hubbub of chatter had somehow dropped away or the volume had been switched down low.

And then a little girl rolled her ball under the table and

scrambled under Sarah's chair to find it and the moment was lost.

They finished eating, chatting about the village and how it compared to Silverford

back home, and they headed back into the snow. There was a palpable buzz of excitement – not just from the giddy children who were waiting for the arrival of Christmas Eve tomorrow, but even the parents and the other adults seemed to be caught up in it, too.

"So, the carol service," he said, clearing his throat. "It seems like kind of a big deal around here."

"Oh, it is. It's a chance for everyone to meet up before the big day. And everyone loves carols, don't they? Even if they can't sing."

"I think it brings us back to being kids." He was carrying a bag from the art gallery in one hand, his gloves in the other as they walked back towards the car. The air was crisp, snowflakes still falling gently.

Sarah fished in her bag for the car keys, and he threw his things onto the back seat and pulled on his gloves, clearing off the snow that had fallen from the roof of the car.

"Habit," he explained, as Sarah gave him a questioning look. "You wouldn't believe the number of car wrecks that happen every year because people don't clear their cars."

She tipped her head with a smile. "Not something we really have to think of here in Applemore. It's more likely to be floods than snowstorms most winters."

He climbed into the car, following her lead, and they waited a moment as the wipers cleared away the last flakes of snow.

"So—" he began.

"Are you—" she said.

They laughed and he gestured with an open hand. "After you."

"I was going to say – maybe I'll see you there."

He took off his hat and ran a hand through his hair, feeling a broad smile spreading across his face.

"I'd like that."

They headed back towards Applemore, Sarah pulling up outside the hotel for a moment with the engine still running. On the other side of the street, last minute preparations were being made around the big tree by the harbour.

"Looks like it really is a big deal."

"Oh, just you wait." She grinned, eyes sparkling.

"I'm looking forward to it."

"Me too." He leaned on the open door and looked in at her for a moment. "I'll see you later."

"It's a date." Sarah put a hand to her mouth, her face flushing pink in an instant. "I mean it's a deal."

"See you later, Sarah." Jim closed the door and lifted his arm in a wave as he stood on the snowy street, watching as she drove away before he headed in through the sparkling archway of greenery that hung over the doorway of the Applemore Hotel.

7

SARAH

Even after showering, washing and drying her hair, trying on several outfits and then telling herself firmly that she was going to be wearing a winter coat and scarf, so it didn't matter what she had on, Sarah's face was still glowing as if she'd been wired up to the mains.

They weren't going to need lights on the Christmas tree by the harbour because her mortification at saying *it's a date* was so complete that she was capable of illuminating the entire village.

She checked the time – quarter to seven – and forced herself to sit down on the arm of the sofa for five minutes just to be sure she didn't get there early and look overly keen.

Then the car – always temperamental – decided that tonight was the night it was going to refuse to start.

"Don't do this to me," she muttered, closing her eyes and counting to three before trying the engine again. On the third attempt it spluttered into life, and she drove down the hill into Applemore, where the main street was lined with cars and the pavements packed with people, all heading in one direction. She joined the crowd and was carried along, trying to look casual as she got closer. Perhaps Jim would have decided against it – researching small towns, he'd probably seen a million of these little events on his travels.

But no, there he was, his height and upright posture meaning he stood out in the crowd. His eyes met hers and his face broke into a warm smile as he started to move towards her.

"Hi there," he said, stepping back as a gaggle of teenagers rushed past, laughing and waving bright glow-sticks. "You weren't kidding when you said everyone would be here." He passed her a cup. "I got you a cup of hot apple cider."

It smelled spicy and delicious, a piece of star anise bobbing on the top. She sipped it and looked around, her arm brushing against his as the crowd gathered and everyone pressed themselves against the rails of the little harbour.

"Hi, Sarah," a voice said. She turned to see Charlotte Fraser, a paper cup in each hand, giving her a smile. "I swear this gets busier every year."

Sarah watched as Charlotte flicked a glance in Jim's direction and then – her face hidden by the side-sweep of straw-berry-blonde hair – raised her brows to express interest. Her mouth curved in the beginnings of a smirk and then she headed off into the crowd.

"I guess knowing everyone," Jim said, leaning in so he could be heard over the chatter of voices, "is part and parcel of running a café in the middle of a small town."

"There isn't much that happens here in Applemore that goes un-noticed, you're right."

"A blessing and a curse, huh?"

She laughed. "Something like that."

The carols were heartwarming as ever, the tiny children from the nursery school singing a song with little tinsel halos looped around their heads.

Their breath rose in the air as they sang along with the old familiar tunes, watching as Greta and Dolina bustled about making sure everything ran smoothly.

"Looking forward to our meeting tomorrow," Dolina said to Jim as she handed Sarah a basket of slim white candles. "I'm giving you these," she added. "Can you just pass them around as we get started?"

"Of course."

Jim bent to pick up one of the candles that fell as she tried to juggle the basket and her paper cup.

"Let me take that." His gloved finger brushed against hers as he took the cup out of her hands and stacked it inside his. Sarah took a long slow breath in, trying to gather herself.

As the familiar tune began, she felt the hairs at the back of her neck rising. There was something about *Silent Night* that always made her want to cry. She turned to her neighbour, catching the flame from her candle, and then passed the basket to Jim. He took one, touching the wick against hers, the flame illuminating his face.

Her eyes met his for a moment and they turned back to face the Christmas tree, singing the lines she'd heard every year since she was a little girl, standing in front of the tree with her own primary school classmates.

For a moment she thought of Tor, sunning himself in Morocco, and her mother, and how much she'd love to see the café thriving and doing well. She slid a sideways glance at Jim, his profile silhouetted against the glow of the streetlamp, and wondered if he, too, was thinking of Christmases past.

As always, as soon as the final carol ended the crowd

thinned out almost instantly, parents rushing their over-tired children off to bed and people heading into the Applemore Hotel, keen to get a table at the bar before it got too busy. She stifled a yawn, suddenly tired after her early start.

"Can I walk you back to your car?"

"Oh," she said, about to protest that she'd be fine and then snapping her mouth shut for a second. She nodded once. "That would be very nice, thank you."

"You must have a pretty good picture of what makes Applemore tick by now." She squeezed through the gap in two parked cars as he stood aside.

"Yes, I think so. However, I don't believe my research will be complete until tomorrow."

The swoop of disappointment in her stomach was so unexpected that she pressed a hand to her body as if to contain it. "You're leaving tomorrow?"

Jim laughed. "Not at all. I have a very important meeting at mid-day."

"Oh, of course." She shook her head, laughing. "How could I forget. The second half of Dolina's information download."

"Yes." Jim's tone was dry, and his mouth twisted in a half-smile. "I'm sure it will be... illuminating."

Sarah giggled. "Well, I'll be sure to keep an eye out. Give me a sign if you need to be rescued."

"I would appreciate that very much."

They arrived at the car, and she dug in her bag to find the keys. Jim glanced across at the dark sea, frowning in thought.

"And you'll be giving Chloe her last-minute tips for Christmas dinner, I guess."

"I'm hoping she's got everything under control by now. Are you—what are you doing on Christmas Day?"

"Me?" Jim grinned. "Well, I've got some very important research to be getting on with, but other than that—well, there's dinner at the hotel, but I think dinner for one might feel a little uncomfortable. I might skip it altogether in favour of some room service."

There was a beat of silence, broken only by the distant sound of laughter and a call of, "Have a good Christmas" as the last of the crowds headed home.

"And you?" Jim said eventually.

"I'm not—" Sarah bit her lip, her heartbeat rushing in her ears as she tried to pluck up courage. "I'm don't have any plans, actually," she said, trying to sound airy. "I might go for a walk, actually, if you want to join me?" She gave a little laugh, as if the idea was completely ridiculous.

Jim's mouth turned up in a slow smile.

"I'd like that very much, Sarah."

"You would?"

"I would."

"Okay," she said, flustered, "That's great. Lovely. I'll—I'd better get going. I've got an early morning ahead of me."

"I'll see you at mid-day," he said in his deep accent. And he stepped towards her for a moment, hands lifting.

For a moment she thought he was going to hug her, but he shook his head slightly, almost laughing, and raised his chin with a rueful look on his face.

"I had a good night, thank you."

"I did too."

"Goodnight, Sarah," he said, turning as she pulled open the car door.

"Goodnight, Jim," she said, smiling to herself. Whatever this was, it was an awful lot nicer than the normal run-up to Christmas.

She turned the key in the ignition, sending up a little peti-
tion of thanks when the engine started first time.

8

SARAH

There was something about the magic of Christmas Eve that never faded, even in adulthood, long after you knew that the magic was not in fact coming from the man at the North Pole. The harried women – who were usually in charge of the magic that happened – had been rushing in and out of the café, picking up gingerbread orders, and panic buying last minute gifts. Sarah had been up since 3 a.m. baking a double batch, knowing that whatever she'd baked for the orders wasn't going to be enough.

The snow had stopped, frozen in place by a hard frost which had sparkled on the car that morning when she'd climbed out of bed in warm pyjamas and peered outside as the kettle boiled.

The coffee machine was hissing and steaming behind her as she rang up another of the gingerbread orders. It made her heart happy to see the café full on Christmas Eve, knowing it was a haven where people could get away for an hour or so and take a break from the rush. The tables were full.

"Can you check the recycling bin and stick it out the back

please, Mollie?" Sarah called over her shoulder to one of the teenagers who was helping out, making some extra money in the holidays when they needed staff.

"I will do. How come there are so many dads and children in here today?" she asked, frowning at Sarah as she stood in the doorway. "It's weird."

Sarah shook her head, laughing. "Not weird at all." She rearranged the cookies on the glass shelf under the counter, then straightened up, stretching her back, which was aching. "Right now, I can tell you that the wives are at home, frantically wrapping presents and getting things organised for tomorrow. They've been banished from their houses."

"Oh," said Mollie, nodding slowly. "How come it's always the mothers that have to do all that stuff?"

Sarah shot her a knowing look. "I could tell you it's not always, but the reality is if you went up to the North Pole, I can guarantee you that Mrs Claus would be the one doing all the hard work behind the scenes while the man in red takes all the credit."

"Hmm."

"Well, yes. Let's just say we've got a long way to go, equality wise." Sarah rolled her eyes, laughing. "Where's Chloe, by the way?"

"I'm here." Wiping her hands on a towel, she popped her head around the door. "I was just clearing up and checking something."

"Turkey related, by any chance?" Sarah and Mollie exchanged glances. Chloe's obsession with creating the picture-perfect Christmas dinner was a running joke with everyone in the café.

"As it happens, yes." Chloe pouted. "Do you think I

should baste it? Some people say yes, and others say just cover it in organic butter and that's enough."

"This turkey's had the equivalent of a spa holiday. You've had it brining in white wine and spices and now you're covering it in expensive butter."

"It cost enough." Chloe huffed a laugh, shaking her head. "Apparently there's a real taste difference between organic ones and the kind you get from the supermarket."

Sarah pressed her lips together and raised her brows. If only Chloe knew Alex's plans, she'd probably be worrying more about what she should be wearing for the inevitable engagement photographs she'd be putting on Instagram, and less on the world's most pampered turkey.

"I'm sure it's going to be delicious whatever happens." Sarah raised a hand in greeting as Sophie, the vet, opened the door, pulling off her winter hat and shaking her hair loose.

"Maybe I should put the oven temperature up a bit to make up for opening the door?"

"Hi Sophie, what can I get you?" Sarah said, gratefully.

Chloe popped out just before mid-day to grab some things from the little supermarket and double check on her vegetables, leaving Sarah leaning against the door, breathing a sigh of amused relief. The girls were busy clearing up in the lull, stacking plates and mugs into the dishwasher and wiping down tables. It looked like the rush might be over. She turned the music channel over from the Christmas tunes that had taken residence in her brain and checked her phone to see a string of messages from Tor.

Having a great time – you'd love it here!

There was a photo of him lying on a sunbed by a

turquoise pool, the sky overhead such a bright blue that it looked as if someone had turned up the colours on the image. Her brother was holding a cocktail in one hand and a novel in the other – she zoomed in on the image to see what on earth he was reading.

> Flora Douglas? Isn't she the writer from Applemore?

His reply came back a moment later.

> Oh yeah, I think so. Saw it in the airport and thought I might try reading something instead of sitting on my phone all week.

She grinned at the thought of her builder brother, who was normally flat out working six days a week to keep up with demand, lying by a pool with a book and a pina colada. She shook her head, still laughing as she put her phone back in the back pocket of her jeans.

The bell rang and she looked up. Alex, a thick woollen beanie hat pulled down low on his forehead, was standing in the doorway. His huge blue tractor was parked on the road outside. The little girl sitting by the window stood up on her chair and peered out, her face pressed up against the glass.

"Look, Daddy, a tractor!"

"Sarah," Alex said, covering the floor in three long strides. His eyes darted from side to side. "Chloe about?"

She shook her head, lifting the end of a string of fairy lights which had come unstuck and fixing them back into place. "She's popped out to the shops – she'll be back in a moment."

He looked alarmed, his eyes widening. "Och no, I'm not

looking for her – I wanted to have a word. Does she seem alright to you?"

"Chloe?" Sarah scratched her head. "Yeah, she's fine. Just stressed about this turkey, I think."

He gave a sigh. "Thank goodness. I was worried for a wee minute there. I thought maybe she'd gone off the idea of..."

"No." Sarah gave him a reassuring smile. "She's doing all this for you. She wants to make your first Christmas dinner in the house perfect. And I'm sure it will be."

"Well, that's a relief. I'd better get off. I've got to move the cows down to the inbye field for the weekend."

"No rest for the wicked, hey?" Sarah laughed.

"You and me both," Alex said, giving a wave of farewell.

"You and me both," Sarah echoed to herself, half an hour later. The lull had been replaced with an influx of customers, who'd arrived in a wave as if they'd come in en masse from an event elsewhere.

"And five pieces of shortbread," she said, passing over a paper bag. She looked up as the door opened, her heart giving a little leap when she realised that the broad-shouldered shape silhouetted in the bright mid-day sun was Jim. He stepped aside to allow two women out, then walked towards her, smiling.

He'd opened his mouth when he turned as someone grabbed his arm from behind.

"There you are."

Dolina's unmistakable tones rang out and he turned around to greet her instead. Sarah, reminding herself that she didn't have any right to feel disappointed, busied herself with work. Chloe returned, looking even more frazzled than she had before, and got to work immediately, serving Jim and

Dolina so she didn't even have the excuse to go over and say hello.

At least tomorrow they'd have time to talk. Eventually, half an hour later, he caught her eye, pen in hand as Dolina – who hadn't stopped talking since she arrived – was waggling a finger as she made a point. His eyes widened slightly, and he raised his brows.

"You're on your own," she mouthed at him, making him smile. A moment later he came up to the counter, pulling out his wallet.

"Hi," Jim said, mouth curving in a slow smile.

"Leaving so soon?" Sarah checked his bill.

"Dolina's taking me on a tour."

9

JIM

Sarah looked as if she could do with someone to run her a hot bubble bath, light her a fire, and hand her a glass of wine. Her hair was coming loose from the red velvet ribbon she'd tied around her ponytail, and her apron looked as if she'd lost a fight with a bag of icing sugar.

"What kind of tour?" She tore off the receipt and handed it to him, her fingers brushing his for a moment.

He pulled in a breath, feeling like a teenager. This was a ridiculous state of affairs.

"She's taking me up to the village hall, apparently."

"Oh, that's a good idea." Sarah bent down, lifting a couple of heavy bags up from underneath the counter. "Would you mind dropping these off for me? I was going to do it after we'd closed, but I think it might make more of a difference now."

"Sure thing."

"It's some extra packs of gingerbread, shortbread biscuits, things like that. We always take our leftover bakery produce up to the community cupboard at the village hall at the end of the day, but everyone's going to be so busy today I worry that it'll spoil. This way people can get what they need for tomorrow."

"Okay," he said, frowning. "I'm sure all will become clear shortly."

"Come on," said Dolina, bustling over and hooking him by the elbow. She looked over at Sarah with a fond smile. "I'll speak to you later, my love. Are you quite sure you don't want to come and have Christmas with us?"

Sarah glanced up at him for a moment through her dark lashes, shaking her head.

"No, definitely not – but thanks Dolina, I've got a quiet day planned. I've been working so hard I'll be glad of the rest."

"Well, if you change your mind, you know where we are."

"I do."

"Right then, let's go. You've got a little hire car, yes?"

Jim nodded and pulled the keys out of his pocket. "I have, it's parked outside the hotel."

"Well, that sounds like a better idea than walking all the way up the hill when it's so icy outside. At least they've gritted the roads."

Dolina clung onto his arm as they made their way along the pavement towards the hotel. The pavements had been given a fresh coating of red salt and snow crusted the edges, stained slightly with the to-ings and fro-ings of a busy day in the village. The piles of slightly grubby snow reminded him of back home in New England. Snow shovelling was part of winter life there, and snow was a fact of life rather than a romantic addition. Here it was a constant source of wonder and entertainment, and the British preoccupation with the weather amused him.

"More snow tonight, can you believe," Dolina said, making him smile.

"I do seem to have brought the weather with me," he said, opening the car door for her. "Sorry, I'm afraid it's a little chilly in there."

His breath hung in the air.

"Oh, I'm nice and warm in my coat, don't worry." Dolina strapped herself in and looked at him expectantly.

"Which direction are we headed?"

She chuckled. "Sorry, I completely forgot you don't know your way around. Up the road here and take a left as the road forks. The community centre is at the top of the hill, by the fire station."

"We all do our bit, here," Dolina explained when they got to the community centre. "It started with the Lighthouse Library – people would leave things they didn't need or had too much of. Of course, Kathleen – she was the start of it. She used to take eggs down every day, rain or shine. And we have our share of poverty here in the village and the surroundings. It's no' all fancy houses and holiday cottages."

"Rural poverty is a real concern everywhere."

"Even over there where you are?" Dolina waved an arm in the general direction of the west.

"Very much so." He opened the back door and pulled out the bags that Sarah had given him. "People like Sarah who give their leftover goods make a real difference."

Inside the community centre a gaggle of excited children were playing a game, marshalled by two older women wearing Santa hats. The hall was warm and cosy, and in the corner, there was a circle of chairs and some people drinking hot drinks.

"We've got a warm space here, so nobody has to worry

about their heating bills," Dolina said, leading him to a big wooden cupboard. An elderly man in a cardigan decorated with candy canes appeared out of a doorway, holding a clipboard.

"I'm just showing Jim around," Dolina said, puffing up her chest. "We've got some bits and pieces here from the café."

He took the bag, tucking the clipboard under his arm. "I'll get that noted, Dolina, thank you. We're expecting some of the service users in later on, so this is perfect timing."

"So, as you can see," Dolina continued, "this place plays a big part in Applemore. Jobs are coming up all the time as the place expands and more and more places are opening up, but you can't wave a magic wand, can you?"

Jim was touched at how passionate she was. Applemore – like countless other small towns he'd come across on his travels – was held together by the kindness of people like Dolina. They might seem gossipy or suspicious about incomers, but at the end of the day they looked out for the less fortunate. He had a huge affection for the Dolinas of this world.

She looked at her watch. "Would you look at the time. I really better get on. No doubt my daughter Jenny still has a mountain of presents to wrap."

They got back to the car and discovered a couple of packs of gingerbread men had slipped down the side of the chair.

"I'll take them in," Jim said. "Don't worry. You get into the car, and I'll take you home."

When he returned, Dolina was looking thoughtful, her brow furrowed.

"Is everything okay?" He switched on the engine.

"Oh yes." She nodded. "I was just thinking. Isobel would

be so proud of what Sarah's done with the café. But talking to you – I worry she's buried herself here."

He lifted his head, looking at her steadily as his pulse quickened.

"What do you mean?"

"Well, Sarah was always the dreamer of the twins. Tor was the one who was happy here in Applemore – well, happy enough until he got divorced, I suppose. And now he's off gadding about in Morocco. I think she feels like she can't leave because she's responsible for keeping up her side of the bargain."

"Running the café, you mean?"

Dolina nodded. "I think she needs someone to give her the nod. Tell her it's okay if she wants more than just running the café." She gave him a knowing look.

He met her eye but said nothing.

"Anyway," Dolina said, pursing her lips and folding her arms over her capacious bosom. "Of course that's nothing to do with me, and I'm no' one for sticking my nose in other people's business."

He had to disguise the laugh that tried to escape with a fit of coughing, and the next thing Dolina was rooting around in her bag.

"I've got some cough sweets in here," she said, as they headed down the hill and into the village.

Despite his protestations, she gave him a handful before he dropped her off outside her little house on the edge of the village. He drove back to the hotel, lost in thought. The windows of the Applemore Hotel were glowing, candles dancing in their metal holders. Inside, he could see shapes moving around and hear the distant sound of Christmas music being played by a band. Maybe he'd order room service instead of eating downstairs and see if he could Face-Time Laurel in Madagascar. He felt a strange mix of anticipation for tomorrow, and a sense of something alongside it that he couldn't quite name. Was it... guilt?

That was it. Upstairs, he scrolled through the photos on his phone, realising just how far back he had to go now to find the last images of Meg. There she was, smiling at him with that funny, teasing half-smile she had.

He could hear her voice in his head.

"Pull yourself together, my love. I told you to go on living. That's exactly what this is."

Funny that the advice his wife would have given echoed what Dolina had said earlier. It felt strange to have an insight into Sarah's life that she might not even have acknowledged herself. He picked up the room service menu and shrugged off his coat. Tomorrow was Christmas Day, and for the first time in years he had a reason to look forward to it.

10

SARAH

The very last thing she expected to do on Christmas Day was sleep late. The 5:30 a.m. wakeup call was so ingrained in her brain that even on the days that Chloe was doing the morning shift her body clock would see her up and making coffee in the winter darkness. Maybe it was the quiet outside? She pulled back the curtains to see that the forecast snow had fallen overnight, and Applemore was blanketed once more in sparkling white.

This was the one day of the year where everyone seemed to stand still – no tyre tracks in the snow, no postie waving cheerfully through the window as she delivered the letters in her brightly coloured coat. Sarah – who normally appreciated the peace and quiet of her little cottage, after a long and busy working day full of people – found herself switching on the radio.

"And a very Merry Christmas to anyone out there who happens to be spending the day alone – we're here to keep you company all day long, so why not grab a slice of

Christmas cake, pour yourself a drink and settle down for a morning of your favourite seasonal songs!"

"No, thank you," she said, switching off the radio as Mariah Carey started to warble. "All I want for Christmas is not to have to listen to any more Christmas music."

She headed upstairs for a shower, switching it on and looking at herself in the mirror as the steam started to fog the glass. *Hair up or hair down*? She caught her dark waves in her hand and lifted them up, wrinkling her nose. Either way, it was going to get squashed flat under a hat. She still hadn't worked out where to go with Jim and her stomach fluttered with anticipation at the thought. Maybe they could take a drive up to the waterfall. It would be pretty in the snow, and it was the one day of the year it wouldn't be crowded with tourists taking photographs.

A couple of hours later she walked down to the café, wrapped up against the cold in her red hat and scarf. Butter-flies were crashing around in her stomach, which she told herself was ridiculous. All she was doing was doing a good deed for another person at a loose end on Christmas Day. If Tor had been there, she'd have invited Jim to join them, after all. So, it was nothing more than a kind gesture – but that didn't explain why, when she'd had a call from her brother just as she was drying her hair after her shower, she hadn't mentioned what she was doing.

"Hi there," Jim said, walking out of the doorway of the Applemore Hotel just as she arrived. He had the keys for his hire car in one hand, his leather gloves in the other. "Where are we headed?"

They drove out of the village and over the top of the hills, passing the black and white cows gathered around a feeder full of hay, their breath hanging in white clouds.

"You see, we're not the only ones skipping Christmas." Jim laughed, then turned down the single-track road on Sarah's direction.

"I hate driving in snow, but you don't seem to mind at all."

He lifted a shoulder in a half-shrug. "Comes with the territory. I learned to drive in it – my birthday is January fifteenth, so as soon as I turned fifteen, I was out in my dad's truck."

"You can drive with gears as well, though?" Sarah looked down at his hand.

"We call it driving stick over in the States." He flexed his fingers. "Yeah, my dad was old-school. Said that if I was learning, I had to do it properly."

"He sounds strict."

"Strict but fair." Jim glanced over at her. "He got the balance right, I think."

"Is he—" Sarah stalled on the word for some reason, raising her brows in query instead, then quickly added, "Oh, this is it just here. If you pull up at this gate, you'll see the parking place."

"Oh yeah, he died when I was forty. Heart attack, which was the best way to go." He gave a rueful smile. "There's no way he'd have coped with being nursed. He couldn't stand fuss."

"Sounds like my mother." She unclipped her seatbelt and climbed out of the car.

"Yeah, the apple didn't fall far from the tree in my case." He slid her a sideways look as he closed his door. "Or yours, I'm guessing."

Sarah laughed and gestured towards a narrow wooden gate, piled with fresh snow. "Good guess. It's this way."

"So where are you taking me on this beautiful Christmas

Day?" Jim stood aside, holding open the gate as she passed through ahead of him.

"The Blackwater Waterfall. It's down the path through these trees – we follow the path of the river, and then—well, you'll see."

"I'm intrigued."

"It's not really relevant to your research, I'm afraid."

He smiled and his arm brushed against hers as the path narrowed.

"Although," she continued, "I suppose they have some effect on the economy because we get lots of visitors coming – especially now. They come and take photos for their social media accounts – like Instagram and YouTube and all of that."

He put a hand on her arm, and she stopped in surprise.

"I came out with you today because I like your company, Sarah, not because I wanted a chance to get some more work done."

Her lips parted and she took in a breath of surprise. Somewhere underneath her thick winter coat her heart did a little skip.

"Oh," she managed after a moment.

"It's a long time since I've—" he began.

And then the shrill sound of her phone rang out, making her jump in surprise. She pulled it out of her coat pocket and looked at the screen, shaking her head in amusement.

"It's Chloe. Excuse me, I'd better answer this." She pulled off a glove to tap the screen and accepted the call.

"Yes," she said, laughing. "I do think you should add some extra bay leaves to the gravy."

"Oh Sarah," came a howl of despair, "I've ruined it. I've ruined Christmas."

11

SARAH

"What do you mean you've ruined Christmas?"

Jim looked on, his head cocked in concern.

Chloe's words tumbled out without a space for breath. "The new oven. I didn't read the signs properly – they're not words, just little pictures. Anyway, I did everything right – the brine, the butter under the skin, the whole thing. It looked amazing. Then I wrapped it in a blanket of foil—"

"Okay," Sarah said, trying to calm her down. "That all sounds perfect."

"And then I-I put it in the oven, and it didn't seem to be all that hot, but I thought, 'oh well, it'll heat up, I've got ages.' Only I had a peek just now and it's still cold on the bottom and the top is all crispy and almost burnt under the foil."

Jim took off his hat and ran a hand through his hair. Sarah looked at him, wordlessly.

"I just wanted everything to be lovely," Chloe wailed. "I know you're having a no-Christmas-Christmas, but I don't suppose you'd—"

Sarah looked at Jim and took a deep breath. "Of course I will. Give me ten minutes and I'll be with you."

"I need you to help me out without Alex seeing. I don't want him thinking I've messed it up. If his mum gets wind of it, I'll never hear the end of it – you know what she's like."

"I'll creep in the back way, don't worry. Like a crack turkey rescue squad."

Chloe gave a little giggle.

"I'll be there ASAP."

Wordlessly, Jim turned around and together they started walking back up towards the car park.

"I'm sorry to ruin your walk," Sarah said, after a couple of minutes.

"Oh, we can walk anytime," Jim said with a chuckle. "It's not every day that there's a Christmas proposal at stake."

"And to think she's worried about the turkey." Sarah laughed. "What on earth has she done?"

"By the sounds of it—" Jim began.

"You got the gist?"

"It wasn't hard."

"She can be quite..." Sarah looked for the word.

"She'd have been great on the stage." Jim laughed. "Very good projection."

"Strident is the word I was looking for. You're a lot more diplomatic than I am."

"Oh, I don't know. I've watched you dealing with various crises over the last few days and you seem to take it all in your stride. And you've got Dolina wrapped around your little finger, which is pretty impressive from where I'm standing."

They climbed into the car and headed back down the empty roads towards Applemore. A tractor passed ahead of them at the crossroads, a huge round bale of hay speared on the prongs in front of it. The old farmer in the cab raised a hand and gave a nod, frowning in surprise to see someone else out on the roads.

"Looks like the cows are getting their Christmas Day meal on time."

"Let's hope I can sort this. I'm sorry I've had to—"

Jim put a hand on her knee, resting it there for a moment. She felt the heat through the fabric of her jeans, wondering as she took a breath why the heat seemed to have risen directly to her cheeks which she could feel going pink.

"I'm coming with you."

"You are?"

Jim laughed. "I wouldn't miss this for the world. Now, you can call this research if you like, but I want to know what she's done to that turkey."

They were still laughing when they crested the hill and Applemore came into sight.

"It's the little row of new houses there," she said, pointing.

12

JIM

Jim pulled the car up on the road behind a row of tiny, box-like little houses. Each one had a wooden fence surrounding it, and he could see the glow of lights at each window.

"It's this one," Sarah said, catching his elbow as she led him to the furthest house. "We can sneak in the back way. I'll text Chloe and tell her we'll be there in a sec."

He watched her pausing for a second, biting her lip as she tapped a quick message onto the screen and then pocketed her phone.

"Okay. Let's go."

He lifted the latch on the wooden gate, and they slipped inside, creeping down the garden path to the back door of the house. Colourful lights were twinkling at the window, and inside he could see a neat kitchen with a shiny, very high-tech looking oven on the wall.

Sarah knocked very softly on the door and then looked back at him for a moment.

"I think we should just sneak in," she said, hand on the

doorhandle. "She knows we're coming. I guess she's probably distracted Alex somehow."

And then they saw what was happening in the hallway. Alex – dressed smartly in a pair of dark jeans and a shirt – was on one knee, and Chloe – wearing an apron, her hair mussed up and anything but picture-perfect – was standing with a hand over her mouth, the tears falling from her eyes nothing to do with the uncooked turkey waiting in the kitchen.

Jim put a hand on Sarah's shoulder, and she turned to look at him, tears filling her eyes. For a moment he ached to pull her into his arms, and then common sense took over.

"I think we should probably—" he began, but Alex, sensing their presence, turned around at exactly that moment and sprung to his feet, somehow managing to embrace Chloe and beckon them inside at the same time.

"She said yes!"

He was grinning broadly. Chloe was wiping away tears with her right hand and holding out her left, examining the way her brand new ring sparkled in the light.

"Oh Sarah, look," she said, rushing forward into her arms.

Jim stood back, not quite sure what to do with himself.

"Come in, man," Alex said in his Highland accent. "Come and have a drink. We've got something to celebrate!"

They headed into the kitchen, where Sarah took a look inside the oven as Alex found some glasses and passed over a bottle of champagne.

"Can you open that please, mate?"

Jim unwrapped the foil and twisted off the wires as Sarah turned the oven knobs and counted on her fingers, thinking out loud as she did some calculations.

"So basically, you've grilled the turkey." She laughed, putting an extra layer of foil on top of the bird. "If you put it back in the oven – now the oven is actually on – it'll be ready in a few hours. It might not be perfect, but—"

"Perfection is over-rated," Alex said, laughing. "I had the whole proposal worked out and then I walked into the kitchen and found this one in tears."

"And the next thing I know..." Chloe wiggled her left hand, the diamond on her finger sparkling in the light.

Jim smiled at them as he popped open the champagne. Alex passed around the glasses, still grinning from ear to ear.

"You can do dinner American style," Sarah told Chloe, laughing. "I don't think they have it at lunchtime over there, do you?"

"We eat at 5 p.m., you're right." Jim watched as Sarah put her arm around Chloe, giving her a loving squeeze. There was something about her kind nature which made his chest feel warm inside – but he couldn't help thinking about Dolina's words yesterday. She was there for her friends and the community, she was working her fingers to the bone to make sure that the café was a warm and welcoming space for everyone in Applemore, but at what cost?

"To imperfect Christmases," Alex said, touching his glass against Chloe's, "and my beautiful wife to be." He pulled her close, his arm wrapped around her waist. Chloe looked up at him, tired, dishevelled and radiant with love.

They shared a drink, and after a few minutes of chat Chloe reached for the bottle, ready to top up their drinks. Jim shook his head, putting a hand over the top of his glass.

"I'm driving," he explained. "One half-glass is more than enough for me."

Chloe narrowed her eyes and looked from Alex to Sarah, mouth pursed in a suspicious pout.

"Did you have this all planned?"

Sarah's brows rose. Alex chuckled and tipped his head in acknowledgement.

"I ran the idea past Sarah, I'll admit that."

"We didn't plan the part where we crashed the proposal, and you grilled the turkey by mistake." Sarah laughed. "So no, this isn't quite what we had planned for Christmas Day."

Her eyes met his as she sipped her champagne, smiling behind her glass. It was Chloe's turn to look first from him to her friend.

Jim gave a brief chuckle. "I'm sure we can see the waterfall another time."

"Oh!" Chloe put a hand to her mouth again. "I'm so sorry, you were meant to be going for a nice walk and now we've ruined it. D'you want to stay and have dinner? Or something to eat just now?"

Alex raised the bottle. "How about another drink?"

Sarah looked at Jim for a second for confirmation, shaking her head a second later.

"No, this is your day."

"Aye," Alex said, laughing as he stood up from the sofa, "and no' one we're likely to forget."

"I think we'll keep the grilled turkey as our secret," Chloe said, jabbing him in the chest with a teasing finger. "Otherwise I'll never hear the end of it from your mother."

"Your *mother-in-law*," Sarah said, putting down her glass and standing up.

"Uh-oh," Chloe giggled, pretending to take off the ring. "Is it too late to change my mind?"

After a flurry of hugs and handshakes they headed back

outside, the fresh snow squeaking under their boots as they made their way back to his hire car.

"That was very sweet," he said, as they set off back down towards the village.

"It was. I'm sorry it's a bit late to head back to the waterfall, though." She glanced at the clock on the dashboard. "Every year it surprises me how dark it gets by mid-afternoon."

"Yeah," he rubbed his forehead, "the last thing we want is the mountain rescue team having to come find us when we get lost in a ravine."

Sarah huffed out a laugh. "We don't have many ravines in Applemore. It's a pity you didn't get to see it, though."

"But we've done our good deed for the day instead, I guess." He flicked a glance sideways and saw she was gazing out of the window, lost in thought. She let out a quiet sigh, just audible over the hum of the engine.

"That was quite something," he said gently. "It's brave, isn't it? Taking that leap. Choosing someone."

"I suppose it is." Her voice was low.

Driving on autopilot, he headed down the main street and pulled up the car outside the hotel. Somehow it felt oddly anti-climactic – somehow the interruption had broken the easy flow of the day, and now the fun was over. The prospect of his return flight was looming, and with it the knowledge that he'd have to walk away.

"I think a lot of people are scared to want things," he said after a moment of silence. "Too scared to choose a different life, even when the one they're living isn't quite the right fit."

He glanced over, studying her face in profile for a moment without speaking. Sarah bit her lip and pulled in a long breath, as if she was gathering herself for something.

"Right," she said, a little too brightly. "Well—"

"You know, Sarah," he heard himself saying, his words careful. "You do so much for everyone here. Running the café is wonderful, but your mother—have you ever wondered if this is what she'd want?"

Sarah stiffened, her chin lifting slightly. She didn't turn around.

"What d'you mean?"

He cleared his throat. "Something Dolina said to me yesterday hit home."

She was sitting very still, her face unmoving.

"You're probably right," she said quietly.

"Sarah—"

"No, you're right." Her voice was polite and distant now. He could feel the air between them change, as if someone somewhere had closed a door.

Jim grimaced. "I'm sorry, I've spoken out of turn. I—"

"No," Sarah said, pulling on her gloves, "I'm sure you're right."

The shutters were down now. He tightened his hands on the steering wheel.

"I'm sorry. I just wanted you to know that I—"

"I should probably get going," Sarah said, making a show of looking at her watch. "I'm sure you've got lots of work to do, and" – she opened the car door and climbed out, as if on autopilot – "well, anyway. Merry Christmas. Sorry about the walk."

She didn't quite meet his eyes as she looked back into the car.

And then she was gone, walking down the empty street in the strange midwinter twilight.

He watched as she started walking – not in the direction

of the café – because of course, it was closed. He'd forgotten that she'd be walking back into the village, where her little cottage stood up on the hill. He watched her in the rear-view mirror for a few seconds, then shook himself. He turned the keys to spin the car around and offer her a ride home, but by the time he looked up she'd disappeared out of sight.

13

SARAH

The cottage was warm as she stepped inside, but her cheeks felt numb and frozen. She pulled off her gloves, her hands shaking slightly. The Christmas lights twinkled in the hallway, reflecting in the mirror as she stared unseeing into the glass.

She sat down on the stairs to pull off her boots, once again letting out a heavy sigh.

Too scared to choose a different life.

The worst part was that Jim was absolutely right, and she had absolutely no idea what to do about it.

She was glad to get back to the regular routine the next morning, springing out of bed with the alarm. Applemore might have been silent and empty on Christmas Day, but she knew of old that things would be very different on Boxing Day. Last year she'd had the day off, and Gavin and Tom had opened up at the Farm Shop for anyone who needed an escape from the festivities. But today it was her turn, and she'd flipped open the sign that welcomed in customers ten minutes early. They'd had a steady stream of visitors all morning, tired-looking parents collapsing into chairs and sighing with relief as they soaked up the caffeine and their children gave them a few moments of peace playing with their new toys, or colouring with the little pots of crayons that Sarah put out on each table for her smaller clients.

Outside the snow was thawing, and everywhere seemed to be dripping steadily under a murky grey sky that reflected her mood. Soon it would be New Year, and the relentless pressure to start afresh and become a whole new person would begin.

"Morning," sang Chloe, breaking into her gloomy thoughts. She was waving hello to everyone, left hand in the air for maximum exposure of her ring, and absolutely glowing with joy as she popped in on what was supposed to be her day off. Her joy was contagious, and Sarah found herself brightening as she kept an eye on the door, half-hoping that Jim might take a walk along from the hotel and settle down at the table which she now thought of as his.

They were closing at two thirty, though, and as the time approached there was still no sign of him. She was putting some cups onto a tray when Harry Robertson, owner of the Applemore Hotel, rushed in through the door, his sandy red hair mussed up and a frazzled expression on his face.

He blew a breath upwards, wiping his forehead with the back of his arm.

"Thank goodness you're here."

Sarah laughed. "Where else would I be?"

"That's what Polly said, funnily enough. She said I could

rely on you being here – we've had a sugar crisis. Long story, but you don't happen to have a spare sack of demerara?"

"A sugar crisis?" She raised her eyebrows. "Yes, of course. I went to the wholesaler last week."

"You are an angel." Harry followed her through to the storeroom. "I hear you went off on a jaunt with our American researcher yesterday."

Her stomach contracted.

"Yes," she said as lightly as she could. "Well, that was the plan, anyway. Cupid got in the way—well, Cupid and a kitchen disaster."

Harry grinned. "Seems like they're the theme this Christmas. I bet they didn't spill a can of oil."

"No," Sarah said, laughing again. "No spilled oil, and—well, all's well that ends well."

"I'm intrigued. You'll have to tell me over a coffee next week when things have settled down. You know what it's like – packed all Christmas, then we'll be discounting rooms next week to try and get the place filled up."

She stepped back to let Harry pick up the heavy sack of sugar. He hefted it over his shoulder with a grunt.

"I'm getting too old for this," he said, rolling his eyes. "I need a holiday like Tor. How's he doing?"

"Having the time of his life in Morrocco, according to the messages I woke up to this morning. Although I suspect he might be feeling slightly the worse for wear today."

Harry grinned. "What I would give for a week in the sun."

"You've got Hogmanay to get through first." Sarah ran her hand along the shelf, which was dusty with flour.

"We do. I'm surprised Jim didn't stay to see in the New Year here in Applemore – I told him as he was leaving this morning it's always a bigger deal than Christmas here in Scotland."

He turned to leave, but Sarah couldn't concentrate on what he was saying because the words were still going round in her head.

As he was leaving.

"See you," she said automatically as Harry headed out of the door. The café was almost empty now, and she flipped the sign over to "Closed". It was almost time, anyway.

"Are you sure?" Mollie and Charlie hopped up and down with excitement as she returned to the counter, telling the students they could go home early, and that she'd clear up.

"Of course." She took some money out of the till and handed each of the girls a note. "Go and enjoy yourselves," she said, watching them grab their coats and disappear with almost indecent haste.

The last customer paid up and she cleared up the table, chiding herself. He was leaving anyway, so why on earth had her stomach fallen through the floor when Harry told her he'd left?

She was just putting the milk back in the fridge when she heard a knock at the door. Her heart leapt and she dashed through from the kitchen to see Chloe standing at the window, eyes wide and waving.

"You could look happier to see me," she grumbled, laughing, as Sarah opened the door. "Forgot my purse. Phew, thank goodness it's here on the shelf. I had visions of having lost it somewhere."

Sarah gave a half-hearted smile.

"Thanks again for yesterday. If you hadn't fixed the turkey disaster, I don't know what I would have done."

"Oh, it was nothing, honestly."

"It was," Chloe insisted. "I knew I could rely on you."

Sarah raised her brows in silent acknowledgement, and a sigh escaped from her lips.

"Hey," Chloe said, putting a hand on her arm. "What's up? You okay?"

She nodded quickly. "Yes, yeah. Fine. Just a bit tired, you know?"

Chloe tipped her head sideways and looked at her for a moment, eyes narrowing. "It's more than that, Sar. What's wrong? How was the rest of your day yesterday? Did you go back to the waterfall?"

"No." She turned back to the counter, sliding some pieces of gingerbread from a plate and into a plastic tub. "It was a bit too late. Jim dropped me off and I had a quiet evening."

"Oh." Chloe's voice held a note of disappointment. "I thought you two were really—I mean, the way he looks at you—"

Sarah shrugged. "Well, he's headed back to the states now, so—"

Chloe let go of her arm and stepped back in surprise. "He has? He told me he was here for Hogmanay."

"Plans change, I guess." She snapped on the lid of the tub with more force than necessary.

"I suppose so," Chloe said, resting her elbow on the counter and studying Sarah with a frown. "What happened?" she asked gently after a few moments.

Sarah stared at the floor. "Nothing. He said something, that's all. Something that was probably true, but I didn't want to hear."

"About what?" Chloe's gaze hadn't shifted from her face. "About you staying here?"

Sarah's head snapped up in surprise. "How did you—"

"Oh," Chloe chewed her lip for a moment. "Something Dolina was saying the other day. She mentioned it to me when I was up at the community centre dropping off the bread and cookies. Said she wondered if you felt trapped here because of your mum."

"I'm not trapped—"

Chloe cocked her head. "When's the last time you had a proper holiday? Even Tor's taken a week off and gone to get some sunshine, and he's the biggest workaholic we know."

Sarah's throat tightened. "The café needs me. I—"

"I'm more than capable," Chloe said, folding her arms. "The café needs a manager, not a martyr."

Sarah stepped back. "I'm not a martyr."

Chloe raised both hands in protest. "Okay, sorry, that was a bit strong. But what about that summer school thing you were meant to do the year your mum died?"

"I'd forgotten about that."

She'd had a weeklong art history trip planned, which had been lost in the muddle of grief and trying to keep things going, and somehow she'd forgotten to make the time to reschedule it and the refund money had been absorbed into her bank account and lost along the way.

"Maybe it's time to take a leaf out of your brother's book. I'm more than happy to keep this place going. Take a break, work out what you want from life."

The words hung in the air. Through the window, Sarah could see the harbour, the same view she'd looked at every day for three years. It was beautiful, even as the snow thawed, familiar, and safe.

And suddenly suffocating.

"What did he say to you?" Chloe asked quietly.

Sarah swallowed. "That I was maintaining mum's legacy

instead of actually living. That she'd want me to do more than just... this."

"And?"

"And he was right." The admission felt like something breaking open inside her chest. "He was absolutely right, and I was so angry at him saying it out loud that I shut him down completely."

"Sometimes the truth hurts most when we've been trying not to see it," Chloe said, tipping her head to one side with a thoughtful expression. "Actually, that's pretty good, isn't it? I'm good at this stuff."

Sarah shook her head, laughing. "You are."

"Maybe I should be a therapist."

Sarah shot her a look of alarm.

"Not before you have a holiday, don't worry." Chloe threw her hands in the air, laughing. "Right, I need to go – first official family dinner as fiancée. Wish me luck!"

Chloe rushed off into the pale grey afternoon light, leaving the café empty and Sarah alone with her thoughts.

Clearing up, Sarah noticed every detail where normally she ran through the end of day routine on autopilot. This was her one and only life, and it was time to make some changes.

She thought of Jim, probably at the airport by now – or already in the air, even, on the way back to Vermont where the snow would be falling for the whole of the season, not just for a few magical days. He was heading home to his real life – she'd pushed him away for telling her the truth. And now he was gone.

She moved to the window, looking out at the darkening harbour. The Christmas lights twinkled on the tree, cheerful and oblivious.

Her mother had built this place with love. She'd poured

everything into it in the few months before she died – but she'd built it as a gift to the village, not as a cage for her daughter.

"I don't know what to do," Sarah said out loud to the empty café.

But even as she said it, as she switched off the fairy lights that were strung around the shelves and turned off the cash register and pulled on her coat, she felt as if something had shifted.

Maybe she didn't need to know yet. Maybe the first step was admitting that staying here, exactly as she was, forever but that wasn't the answer, either.

She pulled out her phone and stared at it for a long moment. Then she opened her messages and tapped on Tor's name.

> I think I'm going to take a leaf out of your book and take a break

She hit send before she could change her mind.
The reply came back almost immediately

> Finally! I can recommend Morocco if you're looking for a week off

Sarah took a deep breath and then typed her reply.

> I'm not thinking of a week. I'm thinking of a few months.

Three dots appeared, and then after a moment a message arrived, making her eyes fill with tears.

> Mum would be proud of you, you know

She switched off the lights and pulled the café door closed, leaving it in darkness for the night. Tomorrow she'd talk to Chloe. Tomorrow she'd start making plans.

Tomorrow she'd figure out how to be brave. But tonight, she'd let herself cry for what she'd lost – and for what she still might find, if she was willing to look for it.

14

_____

JIM

"We're expecting a change in the weather," said the voice on the car radio. "Looks like this unusual burst of Christmas weather is back with a vengeance from later on tonight. Snow is forecast for the northwest coast of the Highlands, so what better time to cosy up by the fire and enjoy listening to some of our favourite seasonal tunes."

Jim sighed and looked out at the grey slush that lined the road south. He'd packed up the day before, throwing his things into his leather bag and heading downstairs to tell a surprised Harry that no, he wouldn't be staying for an Applemore New Year after all.

He'd booked a last-minute room in a hotel in Ullapool, telling himself it was a chance to take a look at another small, thriving Highland town. He'd wandered the streets in the rain, visited the castle to find it closed to visitors, and eaten a solitary meal looking out at the damp street before heading upstairs for an uncomfortable night of sleep on a mattress that had seen better days.

Checking out earlier that morning, he'd resolved to head

to Glasgow and check in to the anonymous chain hotel near the airport, return his hire car, and get his head down and focus on work for a few days. Heck, he might even switch his flight and head back to Silverford a few days early.

He drummed his fingers on the steering wheel as the traffic slowed. The funny thing was, he could picture Meg shaking her head in mock despair at him, telling him that he needed to learn to keep his mouth shut sometimes.

"Mansplaining," Laurel would have said, waggling her finger and laughing.

Whatever you called it, he'd stepped out of line. There was a reason why Dolina hadn't broached the subject with Sarah – so why on earth he'd thought it a good idea was beyond him. He had no right to tell her how to live her life.

So now here he was, on the move again, just like he had been for the last five years since Meg died. Never stopping, never investing. Telling himself he was travelling for research, when the truth was it was easier to keep going than it was to stop and allow himself to—

He dashed a hand to his forehead.

All this time studying what makes small people thrive, and the answer was staring him in the face.

It was people, not businesses or buildings. People who chose to invest in the place, to stay and build together. People like Sarah, who did what she did out of a sense of community and care. Like Dolina, who might have her nose in everyone's affairs, but who had a kind heart and wouldn't see anyone go without. Or Harry, who ran the hotel and worked tirelessly to make the place a success. They dug in, stayed put and believed in something. And that was the opposite of what he'd been doing – running, documenting, staying detached. Using his sabbatical as an excuse to avoid his own life.

The traffic started moving and his phone buzzed on the passenger seat.

> Hey dad, I was just thinking about you. You sound happy right now and it makes me happy! Love you!

He felt the familiar warm glow that came whenever his sweet-hearted girl got in touch. They'd worked so hard as parents to fill her with the courage and confidence that had taken her out into the world, following her dream all the way to Madagascar. The irony wasn't lost on him.

Maybe it was time.

As if he was operating on autopilot, his fingers hit the indicator. He swung the car around, turning back at the fork and heading back towards the snow-covered hills which led towards Applemore.

The afternoon light was fading and his heart pounding as he turned down the narrow road that wound down towards the little village by the sea. His heart was pounding when he pulled up outside the hotel, leaving his bag in the trunk as he headed inside. The temperature had dropped since his departure and frost was already sparkling on the metal rails of the harbour.

"Oh hello," said Harry, who standing in the doorway with a crate of beers in his arms. "Forget something?"

"You could say that." Jim gave a half-hearted laugh. "I don't suppose you still have that room free?"

Harry set down the crate and grinned. "As it happens, yes I do. Changed your mind about Hogmanay?"

"Something like that." He followed Jim over to the desk, pulling out his wallet.

"Well, you're in luck. We've got the *ceilidh* tonight..." Harry paused, giving Jim a knowing look. "Everything okay?"

"I hope so." Jim pocketed his room key, already heading back towards the door.

"If you're looking for Sarah," Harry called after him, an artful innocence in his tone, "I happened to spot her a few minutes ago, heading up towards the community centre."

Jim turned to see Harry looking at him with a knowing expression.

"Thanks, Harry."

"Good luck," Harry said, tipping him the ghost of a wink.

15

SARAH

Nothing had changed, and yet everything had. She'd done the same that morning as she did every single day – getting up, shaping the bread, switching on the ovens, and preparing the café for the day. But all of it had been done with a little voice in her head asking the same question over and over again...

You do all this for everyone else, but what are you doing for yourself?

Now, up at the community centre, she had delivered the leftover cakes and bread for the cupboard, and the volunteers were busy bagging them up and scribbling labels on each one with thick black pen. Good bread shouldn't go to waste – people needed it.

But as she headed for the door, she found herself hearing the little voice again, but this time it was asking a question she hadn't allowed herself to consider in years.

When was the last time someone asked what you needed?

"Oh, there you are," Dolina said, coming in the door just

as she was about to pull it open. She rubbed her hands together and shivered. "Cold out there tonight."

"I don't think I've known a winter like this in Applemore."

Dolina shook her head. "It's the coldest we've ever had. No' that the children are complaining, of course. They're over the moon that there's more snow forecast." She cocked her head and looked at Sarah thoughtfully. "How are you doing, love?"

"Oh," she replied, a little too brightly. "Fine, thanks. Looking forward to—"

Dolina – with her unfailing eye for gossip – peered over Sarah's shoulder, standing almost on tiptoe to get a better look.

"Well, well. Looks like your handsome American has come looking for you."

Sarah's heart leapt and she turned around.

Dolina gave her arm a little squeeze and chuckled. "I heard he'd left town. I guess he had second thoughts."

And with that she turned and walked into the community centre, leaving Sarah standing in the doorway with her lips parted as she tried to find words.

Jim walked towards her, his thick dark brows gathered in an expression of concern. She could feel her heart banging against her ribcage and pulled in an unsteady breath, curling her hands into fists by her side.

"You came back," she said after a moment. She wasn't sure if it was a question or an accusation.

He stopped a few feet away, as if he was unsure if he was welcome to come any closer. "I did."

"Harry told me you'd gone."

"Yeah." He gave a rueful smile, rubbing his neck. "And

then I got halfway to Glasgow and realised I'd changed my mind."

Despite everything, Sarah felt the corner of her mouth twitch. "The prospect of an Applemore Hogmanay was too good to resist?"

"Something like that." His eyes held hers. "Sarah," he said, after a moment of silence, "I came back to say I'm sorry. I had no right to—"

"You had every right to tell the truth." She cut him off, surprised by the steadiness in her voice. "That's not why I was upset."

He cleared his throat and shifted his weight from one foot to the other. "Then why?"

"Because I already knew it. And hearing you say it out loud meant I couldn't pretend anymore." She took a breath. The door opened behind her and one of the volunteers stepped outside, passing them with a nod of acknowledgment and hurrying over to their car in the chilly night air.

"I need to head back to the café," she found herself saying. "If you want to follow me down there, we can talk there instead of standing here in the cold."

"I'd like that." He nodded.

Inside the car, she turned the keys in the ignition, watching the lights of Jim's hire car flicker into life in the rearview mirror. What on earth was she doing? Why was he back here?

She drove carefully down the road towards the harbour, aware of the ice that was forming in patches on the tarmac.

The lights of the Christmas tree were sparkling in the darkness, their reflections dancing in the silver baubles that hung from the branches. She pulled the car up to a halt outside the café and a moment later Jim came striding along the road towards her and she climbed out, keys in hand.

"Smells good in here, even at nighttime." Jim took an appreciative sniff as she flicked on the lights. The café was still warm.

"Would you like a drink?" She motioned to the machines, clean and ready for the next day.

"No, thank you." He shook his head. "I would like to apologise properly for speaking out of turn."

"There's nothing to apologise for." Sarah shrugged off her coat and motioned to the table – Jim's table, as she thought of it – and they sat down opposite each other.

"I admire you, Sarah," he said, folding his hands and looking at her directly, his dark eyes meeting hers. "You've got what I've been searching for."

She sat back in her chair, brows raising in surprise. "I have?"

"You have." He nodded. "Roots, purpose. A sense of community. Those things are important. Ironically, it wasn't until I walked away from here – from you – yesterday morning that I realised that I've been so busy studying what makes places like Applemore work that I've been avoiding my own life in the process."

"But you said—"

He shook his head. "I was wrong to tell you how to live your life."

"But you weren't wrong." Her voice was clear and strong as she argued back. "I've been hiding here, telling myself that what I was doing mattered, pretending that I didn't secretly want something more."

"What you're doing *does* matter." He reached out his hand, closing his fingers over hers. They felt warm and heavy against her skin. The simple touch seemed to warm more than her cold hands.

She sat very still as she began to explain. "I'm going to take some time off. Chloe can run this place – in fact it'll do her good to run this place." She laughed. "Maybe it'll keep her mind off obsessing about the wedding. Now she's got the turkey over with, I have a horrible feeling she's got serious Bridezilla potential."

He laughed, and then his expression grew more serious. "Sarah—"

Her pulse quickened at the sound of her name in his deep voice. She bit down on her lower lip, raising her brows as silent encouragement to continue.

"When I left yesterday, I told myself it was because I'd overstepped. That I had no business telling you how to live your life." He looked down at his fingers, spread out now on the table. "The truth is, I was scared."

Her pulse was rushing in her ears. "Scared of what?"

"Of this." He met her eyes. "Of having feelings for someone again. I haven't... since Meg died, I haven't let myself feel anything for anyone. And then I met you."

Her breath caught.

"I've spent the last five years running," he continued, his voice low. "Town to town, study to study. Telling myself it was research, when the truth is I was avoiding going home. Avoiding trying to look at what life might be for me now." He reached out, his fingers touching hers. "And then I came to Applemore and met someone who made me want to stop running."

"Jim—"

He shook his head. "I'm not saying this with any expectation. I just—I needed you to know that what I said to you wasn't just an observation. It was personal. Because I care about you. And I want you to have the life you deserve."

Tears pricked at her eyes as she nodded once. "I-I know. I feel the same way."

Jim's brows lifted and he sat back slightly, taking a long breath in before he spoke.

"So here's what I'm thinking. I go back to Silverford in a few days. Back to teaching in the spring. You take your time off, figure out what you want out of life."

She nodded, not trusting herself to speak.

"But maybe – when you're ready – you could come visit? Spring in New England is beautiful. Everything coming back to life, the trees and the mountains..." His mouth curved into a hopeful smile. "Let me show you my small town. And maybe we can figure out what comes next."

"I'd like that," she managed. "I'd really like that."

She watched as he reached across the table with both hands now, lacing his fingers in his, and then looked up at the café as if she was seeing it for the first time. The sparkling lights that hung around the shelves, the pretty gingham covers on the tables, the sprigs of holly and ivy tucked behind the paintings on the walls.

And then she spoke the words that had been forming in her mind since they'd talked the other day.

"I've realised that I don't have to choose between honouring my mum and living my own life. I can finish my dream my own way."

He smiled at her and squeezed her fingers for a moment, nodding.

"And maybe," he said, low and hopeful, "if I could – I'd like to be a part of that, somehow. If you'll let me."

She looked at him – this man who'd seen her, really seen

her – and not looked away. Who'd told her the truth, even when it hurt. Who'd come back.

"You're staying for Hogmanay?" she asked.

"I'm staying."

"Good." She smiled, and lifted a hand to wipe away a tear. "Then I guess we have a few days to figure things out."

"A few days," he agreed. "And then after that—"

She felt the smile spreading across her face.

Outside the snow had started falling again. But inside the café, under the warm glow of the fairy lights, Sarah felt like for the first time in three years she could breathe again.

EPILOGUE
SARAH

She'd brought the dress two years ago on a trip to Glasgow. It had been hanging in her wardrobe ever since, because in the end, she'd turned down the chance to go to the fancy ball up at Applemore House, giving the ticket to Chloe instead and telling her she didn't mind. It was dark green velvet, with long sleeves and a fitted waist and a low, scooped neckline.

The truth was that she hadn't minded, not really – and it had been the night that Chloe and Alex had finally got together, so it was worth it in the end. And tonight she was going to wear it to see in New Year's Eve at the hotel, with a handsome American as her date. So all in all – she smiled as her reflection in the mirror – she'd call it a win.

There was something magical about this Hogmanay – the promise of new beginnings and a life she'd never expected waiting in the wings. Chloe had told her she looked glowing that morning, and as she rubbed some blusher into her cheeks she looked at her face and realised that maybe her friend was right.

The last few days had felt like a gift. She and Jim had

taken that walk to the waterfall, finally, on a crisp morning when the sun had turned the frozen snow to glittering diamonds. They'd talked for hours – about his life in Silverford, his daughter Laurel and her brave adventures, and about Meg and her mother and the ways that grief had shaped them both.

It felt easy – like slipping into a conversation they'd been having for years, not days.

And tonight was Hogmanay – the biggest celebration of the year here in Scotland. The hotel would be packed with locals and visitors, music and dancing in the countdown to midnight. She'd promised to show him a proper Scottish New Year and promised to show him the steps to Strip the Willow so he didn't embarrass himself on the dance floor in front of the *ceilidh* band.

She grabbed her coat and headed down the hill to the village, her breath clouding in dragon puffs. She carried her shoes in a bag over her shoulder, laughing to herself at what she must look like in a glamorous dress, thick winter coat, and sturdy walking boots. One more spell of snow was forecast for later – it seemed as if this cold spell wasn't quite ready to let go of Applemore just yet.

She kicked off her boots in the doorway of the Applemore Hotel, shoving them into her bag and hanging them and her coat up on the pegs in the porch where they joined countless others.

Inside the hotel had been refreshed, the decorations redone so fairy lights draped every surface and the tree was hanging with silver tinsel. The room was buzzing with laughter and chat.

"Sarah." Chloe waved from across the room, her ring

catching the light. She and Alex were tucked into a corner chatting to Polly Fraser and her sister-in-law, Rilla.

Alex moved towards her, clearing a space with his arm so he she could slip in and join them. After a flurry of greetings, Chloe hooked her arm through Alex's elbow, grinning with the unmistakable look she always sported when she had a secret she couldn't keep.

"What's up?"

Chloe waggled her eyebrows. "We've been talking, and we've decided – we're getting married in June."

"June?" Sarah said in surprise.

"June." Chloe giggled. "We figured, life's too short. Why wait?"

"That's amazing." She hugged her friend.

Life's too short.

The words were still echoing in her head a few moments later as she scanned the room, half listening to the conversation, looking for—

"There you are."

Jim's voice, low and warm, came from behind her. She turned to find him holding two glasses of champagne, looking handsome in a dark blue sweater and jeans.

"You look beautiful," he said as she accepted the glass. His eyes lingered on her for a moment and she felt her cheeks warm.

"Ready to teach me that dance?"

The next hour passed in a blur of music and dancing. Jim was enthusiastic but terrible at *ceilidh* dancing, and they laughed so hard that they were doubled up, their sides aching.

"Don't give up the day job," Dolina said, putting her hand

on Jim's arm. She looked at Sarah with a smile. "You look beautiful, darling. Your mum would be very proud."

"I hope so." Sarah leaned over and gave her a kiss on the cheek. "Thanks, Dolina."

The band played on. The room grew warmer and more chaotic, the bar staff rushing back and forth constantly collecting glasses as they stacked up on the sills beside the fogged-up windows.

And then the uproar quieted slightly as someone shouted, "It's almost time!"

Jim caught her eye and without a word, took her hand and pulled her towards the door, pausing to untangle their coats from the hooks.

The cold air outside hit them with a shock after the warmth outside. Sarah gasped, laughing, as Jim led her away from the hotel and down toward the harbour where the lights were dancing against the blue darkness of the midnight sky.

They reached the harbour rail just as the church bells began to ring out. Midnight. The new year. Inside the hotel she could hear cheering and the opening notes of *Auld Lang Syne*.

Out here it was just the two of them and the softly falling snow and the dark water, reflecting the strings of lights which were strung between the lampposts.

"Happy New Year, Sarah," Jim said softly.

"Happy New Year."

He stepped closer, his hand reaching up to cup her face. His thumb brushed her cheek, and she realised she was trembling – not from the cold, but from anticipation.

"I've wanted to do this since the carol service," he murmured.

She bit her lip as she looked up at him, her eyes meeting his.

"But I wanted to be sure. And I wanted you to be sure, too."

"I am sure." She nodded against his hand.

And then he pulled her close and kissed her, gently at first, as if he was scared she might break. Her hands found the front of his coat and pulled him closer and the kiss deepened into something warmer and more certain, his hand reaching round to tangle in her hair so she gasped against his mouth and felt him laughing in response.

When they finally pulled apart they were both breathless and smiling. Jim's hands framed her face as he looked down at her.

"I'll come to Silverford in spring," she said, raising her chin in determination.

"I would like that very much."

In the sky behind Applemore fireworks were going off, filling the sky with colour. Crowds of people were spilling out onto the pavements to watch, laughing and shouting with their drinks in hand as they celebrated.

But Sarah stayed exactly where she was, holding Jim's hand, looking out at the harbour at the horizon. Out there, far away, was America – and the promise of travel, and adventure, and maybe something more.

A new year, a new beginning. And for the first time in – well, maybe in forever – Sarah was thinking about what *she* wanted, and nothing else.

It was time to start living.

THE END.

. . .

I hope you enjoyed this little novella - it was such fun to write! If you're ready for more from Applemore, I'm delighted to say that The Harbour House - featuring Tor, Sarah's brother, and Flora, a writer who returns to Applemore after leaving thirty years ago at eighteen - will be coming along early in spring 2026.

If you're new to Applemore, you can discover the first in the interconnected standalone Applemore series here - The Winter Cottage

ACKNOWLEDGMENTS

I'd like to say a huge thank you to everyone who reads my books, and who has been excited for more from Applemore. It means more than you know.

With love, Rachael.

ALSO BY RACHAEL LUCAS

Applemore Bay Series

The Winter Cottage

The Flower Farm

Midsummer House

Christmas at Applemore

The Cottage by the Shore

The Lighthouse Library

Auchenmor Island Series

Sealed with a Kiss

Sealed with a Christmas Kiss

Wildflower Bay

Little Maudley Series

The Telephone Box Library

The Village Green Bookshop

Standalone Novels

Finding Hope at Hillside Farm

Coming Up Roses

For Young Adults

The State of Grace

My Box-Shaped Heart

Printed in Dunstable, United Kingdom

MAYBE
Tomorrow

Poems about Time, Doubt, and Becoming

by
Harriet Elston

This book is dedicated to you, the reader

Table of Contents